VITTORIA
Book 1

By

GEORGE MEREDITH

Double 9 Books

Vittoria
Book 1

by **George Meredith**

ISBN: 978-93-57484-87-9

Published by

DOUBLE 9 BOOKS
2/13-B, Ansari Road, Daryaganj
New Delhi - 110002
info@double9books.com
www.double9books.com
Tel. 011-40042856

ABOUT THE AUTHOR

George Meredith OM (February 12, 1828-May 18, 1909) was born in Portsmouth, United Kingdom. He was an English poet, writer, and author, whose books are noted for their intelligence, extraordinary dialogues, and aphoristic way of writing. Meredith's books are also recognised for psychological studies of character and a highly subjective perspective on life that is a long way ahead of its time, considering women are equals to men in all streams. His most popular works are The Ordeal of Richard Feverel (1859) and The Egoist (1879). He was nominated for the Nobel Prize in Literature seven times.

CONTENTS

CHAPTER I
UP MONTE MOTTERONE

From Monte Motterone you survey the Lombard plain. It is a towering dome of green among a hundred pinnacles of grey and rust-red crags. At dawn the summit of the mountain has an eagle eye for the far Venetian boundary and the barrier of the Apennines; but with sunrise come the mists. The vast brown level is seen narrowing in; the Ticino and the Sesia waters, nearest, quiver on the air like sleepy lakes; the plain is engulphed up to the high ridges of the distant Southern mountain range, which lie stretched to a faint cloud-like line, in shape like a solitary monster of old seas crossing the Deluge. Long arms of vapour stretch across the urn-like valleys, and gradually thickening and swelling upward, enwrap the scored bodies of the ashen-faced peaks and the pastures of the green mountain, till the heights become islands over a forgotten earth. Bells of herds down the hidden run of the sweet grasses, and a continuous leaping of its rivulets, give the Motterone a voice of youth and homeliness amid that stern company of Titan-heads, for whom the hawk and the vulture cry. The storm has beaten at them until they have got the aspect of the storm. They take colour from sunlight, and are joyless in colour as in shade. When the lower world is under pushing steam, they wear the look of the revolted sons of Time, fast chained before scornful heaven in an iron peace. Day at last brings vigorous fire; arrows of light pierce the mist-wreaths, the dancing draperies, the floors of vapour; and the mountain of piled pasturages is seen with its foot on the shore of Lago Maggiore. Down an extreme gulf the full sunlight, as if darting on a jewel in the deeps, seizes the blue-green lake with its isles. The villages along the darkly-wooded borders of the lake show white as clustered swans; here and there a tented boat is visible, shooting from terraces of vines, or hanging on its shadow. Monte Boscero is unveiled; the semicircle of the Piedmontese and the Swiss peaks, covering Lake

Orta, behind, on along the Ticinese and the Grisons, leftward toward and beyond the Lugano hills, stand bare in black and grey and rust-red and purple. You behold a burnished realm of mountain and plain beneath the royal sun of Italy. In the foreground it shines hard as the lines of an irradiated Cellini shield. Farther away, over middle ranges that are soft and clear, it melts, confusing the waters with hot rays, and the forests with darkness, to where, wavering in and out of view like flying wings, and shadowed like wings of archangels with rose and with orange and with violet, silverwhite Alps are seen. You might take them for mystical streaming torches on the border-ground between vision and fancy. They lean as in a great flight forward upon Lombardy.

The curtain of an early autumnal morning was everywhere lifted around the Motterone, save for one milky strip of cloud that lay lizard-like across the throat of Monte Boscero facing it, when a party of five footfarers, who had met from different points of ascent some way below, and were climbing the mountain together, stood upon the cropped herbage of the second plateau, and stopped to eye the landscape; possibly also to get their breath. They were Italians. Two were fair-haired muscular men, bronzed by the sun and roughly bearded, bearing the stamp of breed of one or other of the hill-cities under the Alps. A third looked a sturdy soldier, squareset and hard of feature, for whom beauties of scenery had few awakening charms. The remaining couple were an old man and a youth, upon whose shoulder the veteran leaned, and with a whimsical turn of head and eye, indicative of some playful cast of mind, poured out his remarks upon the objects in sight, and chuckled to himself, like one who has learnt the necessity to appreciate his own humour if he is disposed to indulge it. He was carelessly wrapped about in long loose woollen stuff, but the youth was dressed like a Milanese cavalier of the first quality, and was evidently one who would have been at home in the fashionable Corso. His face was of the sweetest virile Italian beauty. The head was long, like a hawk's, not too lean, and not sharply ridged from a rapacious beak, but enough to show characteristics of eagerness and promptitude. His eyes were darkest blue, the eyebrows and long disjoining eyelashes being very dark over them, which made their colour precious. The nose was straight and forward from the brows; a fluent black moustache ran with the curve of the upper lip, and lost its line upon a smooth olive cheek. The upper lip was firmly supported by the under, and the chin stood freely out from a fine neck and throat.

After a space an Austrian war-steamer was discerned puffing out of the harbour of Laveno.

"That will do," said the old man. "Carlo, thou son of Paolo, we will stump upward once more. Tell me, hulloa, sir! are the best peaches doomed to entertain vile, domiciliary, parasitical insects? I ask you, does nature exhibit motherly regard, or none, for the regions of the picturesque? None, I say. It is an arbitrary distinction of our day. To complain of the intrusion of that black-yellow flag and foul smoke- line on the lake underneath us is preposterous, since, as you behold, the heavens make no protestation. Let us up. There is comfort in exercise, even for an ancient creature such as I am. This mountain is my brother, and flatters me not—I am old."

"Take my arm, dear Agostino," said the youth.

"Never, my lad, until I need it. On, ahead of me, goat! chamois! and teach me how the thing used to be done in my time. Old legs must be the pupils of young ones mark that piece of humility, and listen with respectfulness to an old head by-and-by."

It was the autumn antecedent to that memorable Spring of the great Italian uprising, when, though for a tragic issue, the people of Italy first felt and acted as a nation, and Charles Albert, called the Sword of Italy, aspired, without comprehension of the passion of patriotism by which it was animated, to lead it quietly into the fold of his Piedmontese kingship.

There is not an easier or a pleasanter height to climb than the Motterone, if, in Italian heat, you can endure the disappointment of seeing the summit, as you ascend, constantly flit away to a farther station. It seems to throw its head back, like a laughing senior when children struggle up for kissings. The party of five had come through the vines from Stresa and from Baveno. The mountain was strange to them, and they had already reckoned twice on having the topmost eminence in view, when reaching it they found themselves on a fresh plateau, traversed by wild water-courses, and browsed by Alpine herds; and again the green dome was distant. They came to the highest chalet, where a hearty wiry young fellow, busily employed in making cheese, invited them to the enjoyment of shade and fresh milk. "For the sake of these adolescents, who lose much and require much, let it be so," said Agostino gravely, and not without some belief that he consented to rest on behalf of his companions. They allowed the young mountaineer to close the door, and sat about his fire like sagacious men. When cooled and refreshed, Agostino gave the signal for departure, and returned thanks for hospitality. Money was not offered and not expected. As they were going forth the mountaineer accompanied them to the step on the threshold, and with a mysterious eagerness in his eyes, addressed Agostino.

"Signore, is it true?—the king marches?"

"Who is the king, my friend?" returned Agostino. "If he marches out of his dominions, the king confers a blessing on his people perchance."

"Our king, signore!" The mountaineer waved his finger as from Novara toward Milan.

Agostino seemed to awaken swiftly from his disguise of an absolute gravity. A red light stood in his eyeballs, as if upon a fiery answer. The intemperate fit subsided. Smoothing dawn his mottled grey beard with quieting hands, he took refuge in his habitual sententious irony.

"My friend, I am not a hare in front of the king, nor am I a ram in the rear of him: I fly him not, neither do I propel him. So, therefore, I cannot predict the movements of the king. Will the wind blow from the north to-morrow, think you?"

The mountaineer sent a quick gaze up the air, as to descry signs.

"Who knows?" Agostino continued, though not playing into the smiles of his companions; "the wind will blow straight thither where there is a vacuum; and all that we can state of the king is, that there is a positive vacuum here. It would be difficult to predict the king's movements save by such weighty indications."

He laid two fingers hard against the rib which shields the heart. It had become apparently necessary for the speaker to relieve a mind surcharged with bile at the mention of the king; for, having done, he rebuked with an amazed frown the indiscretion of Carlo, who had shouted, "The Carbonaro king!"

"Carlo, my son, I will lean on your arm. On your mouth were better," Agostino added, under his voice, as they moved on.

"Oh, but," Carlo remonstrated, "let us trust somebody. Milan has made me sick of late. I like the look of that fellow."

"You allow yourself, my Carlo, an immense indulgence in permitting yourself to like the look of anything. Now, listen—Viva Carlo Alberto!"

The old man rang out the loyal salutation spiritedly, and awoke a prompt response from the mountaineer, who sounded his voice wide in the keen upper air.

"There's the heart of that fellow!" said Agostino. "He has but one idea —his king! If you confound it, he takes you for an enemy. These free mountain breezes intoxicate you. You would embrace the king himself if you met him here."

"I swear I would never be guilty of the bad joke of crying a 'Viva' to him anywhere upon earth," Carlo replied. "I offend you," he said quickly.

The old man was smiling.

"Agostino Balderini is too notoriously a bad joker to be offended by the comments of the perfectly sensible, boy of mine! My limbs were stiff, and the first three steps from a place of rest reminded me acutely of the king's five years of hospitality. He has saved me from all fatigue so long, that the necessity to exercise these old joints of mine touched me with a grateful sense of his royal bounty. I had from him a chair, a bed, and a table: shelter from sun and from all silly chatter. Now I want a chair or a bed. I should like to sit at a table; the sun burns me; my ears are afflicted. I cry "Viva!" to him that I may be in harmony with the coming chorus of Italy, which I prophetically hear. That young fellow, in whom you confide so much, speaks for his country. We poor units must not be discordant. No! Individual opinion, my Carlo, is discord when there is a general delirium. The tide arriving, let us make the best of the tide. My voice is wisdom. We shall have to follow this king!"

"Shall we!" uttered one behind them gruffly. "When I see this king swallow one ounce of Austrian lead, I shall not be sorry to follow him!"

"Right, my dear Ugo," said Agostino, turning round to him; "and I will then compose his hymn of praise. He has swallowed enough of Austrian bread. He took an Austrian wife to his bed. Who knows? he may some day declare a preference for Austrian lead. But we shall have to follow him, or stay at home drivelling."

Agostino raised his eyes, that were glazed with the great heat of his frame.

"Oh, that, like our Dante, I had lived in the days when souls were damned! Then would I uplift another shout, believe me! As things go now, we must allow the traitor to hope for his own future, and we simply shrug. We cannot plant him neck-deep for everlasting in a burning marl, and hear him howling. We have no weapons in these times—none! Our curses come back to roost. This is one of the serious facts of the century, and controls violent language. What! are you all gathered about me? Oracles must be moving, too. There's no rest even for them, when they have got a mountain to scale."

A cry, "He is there!" and "Do you see him?" burst from the throats of men surrounding Agostino.

Looking up to the mountain's top, they had perceived the figure of one who stood with folded arms, sufficiently near for the person of an expected friend to be descried. They waved their hats, and Carlo shot ahead. The others trod after him more deliberately, but in glad excitement, speculating on the time which this sixth member of the party, who were engaged to assemble at a certain hour of the morning upon yonder height, had taken to reach the spot from Omegna, or Orta, or Pella, and rejoicing that his health should be so stout in despite of his wasting labours under city smoke.

"Yes, health!" said Agostino. "Is it health, do you think? It's the heart of the man! and a heart with a mill-stone about it—a heart to breed a country from! There stands the man who has faith in Italy, though she has been lying like a corpse for centuries. God bless him! He has no other comfort. Viva l'Italia!"

The exclamation went up, and was acknowledged by him on the eminence overhanging them; but at a repetition of it his hand smote the air sideways. They understood the motion, and were silent; while he, until Carlo breathed his name in his hearing, eyed the great scene stedfastly, with the absorbing simple passion of one who has endured long exile, and finds his clustered visions of it confronting the strange, beloved, visible life:—the lake in the arms of giant mountains: the far-spreading hazy plain; the hanging forests; the pointed crags; the gleam of the distant rose-shadowed snows that stretch for ever like an airy host, mystically clad, and baffling the eye as with the motions of a flight toward the underlying purple land.

CHAPTER II
ON THE HEIGHTS

He was a man of middle stature, thin, and even frail, as he stood defined against the sky; with the complexion of the student, and the student's aspect. The attentive droop of his shoulders and head, the straining of the buttoned coat across his chest, the air as of one who waited and listened, which distinguished his figure, detracted from the promise of other than contemplative energy, until his eyes were fairly seen and felt. That is, until the observer became aware that those soft and large dark meditative eyes had taken hold of him. In them lay no abstracted student's languor, no reflex burning of a solitary lamp; but a quiet grappling force engaged the penetrating look. Gazing upon them, you were drawn in suddenly among the thousand whirring wheels of a capacious and a vigorous mind, that was both reasoning and prompt, keen of intellect, acting throughout all its machinery, and having all under full command: an orbed mind, supplying its own philosophy, and arriving at the sword- stroke by logical steps,—a mind much less supple than a soldier's; anything but the mind of a Hamlet. The eyes were dark as the forest's border is dark; not as night is dark. Under favourable lights their colour was seen to be a deep rich brown, like the chestnut, or more like the hazeledged sunset brown which lies upon our western rivers in the winter floods, when night begins to shadow them.

The side-view of his face was an expression of classic beauty rarely now to be beheld, either in classic lands or elsewhere. It was severe; the tender serenity of the full bow of the eyes relieved it. In profile they showed little of their intellectual quality, but what some might have thought a playful luminousness, and some a quick pulse of feeling. The chin was firm; on it, and on the upper lip, there was a clipped growth of black hair. The whole visage widened upward from the chin, though not very markedly before it reached the broad-lying brows. The temples were strongly indented by the swelling of the forehead above them: and on both sides of the head there ran a pregnant ridge, such as will sometimes lift men a deplorable half inch above the earth we tread. If this man was a problem to others, he was none to himself; and when others called him an idealist, he accepted the title, reading himself, notwithstanding, as one who was less flighty than many philosophers and professedly practical teachers of his generation. He saw far, and he grasped ends beyond obstacles: he was nourished by sovereign principles; he despised material present interests; and, as I have said, he was less supple than a soldier. If the title of idealist belonged to him, we will not immediately decide that it was opprobrious. The idealized conception of stern truths played about his head certainly for those who knew and who loved it. Such a man, perceiving a devout end to be reached, might prove less scrupulous in his course, possibly, and less remorseful, than revolutionary Generals. His smile was quite unclouded, and came softly as a curve in water. It seemed to flow with, and to pass in and out of, his thoughts, to be a part of his emotion and his meaning when it shone transiently full. For as he had an orbed mind, so had he an orbed nature. The passions were absolutely in harmony with the intelligence. He had the English manner; a remarkable simplicity contrasting with the demonstrative outcries and gesticulations of his friends when they joined him on the height. Calling them each by name, he received their caresses and took their hands; after which he touched the old man's shoulder.

"Agostino, this has breathed you?"

"It has; it has, my dear and best one!" Agostino replied. "But here is a good market-place for air. Down below we have to scramble for it in the mire. The spies are stifling down below. I don't know my own shadow. I begin to think that I am important. Footing up a mountain corrects the notion somewhat. Yonder, I believe, I see the Grisons, where Freedom sits. And there's the Monte della Disgrazia. Carlo Alberto should be on the top of it, but he is invisible. I do not see that Unfortunate."

"No," said Carlo Ammiani, who chimed to his humour more readily than the rest, and affected to inspect the Grisons' peak through a diminutive opera-glass. "No, he is not there."

"Perhaps, my son, he is like a squirrel, and is careful to run up t'other side of the stem. For he is on that mountain; no doubt of it can exist even in the Boeotian mind of one of his subjects; myself, for example. It will be an effulgent fact when he gains the summit."

The others meantime had thrown themselves on the grass at the feet of their manifestly acknowledged leader, and looked up for Agostino to explode the last of his train of conceits. He became aware that the moment for serious talk had arrived, and bent his body, groaning loudly, and uttering imprecations against him whom he accused of being the promoter of its excruciating stiffness, until the ground relieved him of its weight. Carlo continued standing, while his eyes examined restlessly the slopes just surmounted by them, and occasionally the deep descent over the green-glowing Orta Lake. It was still early morning. The heat was tempered by a cool breeze that came with scents of thyme. They had no sight of human creature anywhere, but companionship of Alps and birds of upper air; and though not one of them seasoned the converse with an exclamation of joy and of blessings upon a place of free speech and safety, the thought was in their hunted bosoms, delicious as a woodland rivulet that sings only to the leaves overshadowing it.

They were men who had sworn to set a nation free,—free from the foreigner, to begin with.

(He who tells this tale is not a partisan; he would deal equally toward all. Of strong devotion, of stout nobility, of unswerving faith and self-sacrifice, he must approve; and when these qualities are displayed in a contest of forces, the wisdom of means employed, or of ultimate views entertained, may be questioned and condemned; but the men themselves may not be.)

These men had sworn their oath, knowing the meaning of it, and the nature of the Fury against whom men who stand voluntarily pledged to any great resolve must thenceforward match themselves. Many of the original brotherhood had fallen, on the battle-field, on the glacis, or in the dungeon. All present, save the youthfuller Carlo, had suffered. Imprisonment and exile marked the Chief. Ugo Corte, of Bergamo, had seen his family swept away by the executioner and pecuniary penalties. Thick scars of wounds covered the body and disfigured the face of Giulio Bandinelli. Agostino had crawled but half-a-year previously out of his Piedmontese cell, and Marco Sana, the Brescian, had in such a place tasted of veritable torture. But if the calamity of a great oath was upon them, they had now in their faithful prosecution of it the support which it gives. They were unwearied; they had one object; the mortal anguish they had gone through had left them no sense for regrets. Life had become the field of an endless engagement to them; and as in battle one sees beloved comrades struck down, and casts but a glance at their prostrate forms, they heard the mention of a name, perchance, and with a word or a sign told what was to be said of a passionate glorious heart at rest, thanks to Austrian or vassal-Sardinian mercy.

So they lay there and discussed their plans.

"From what quarter do you apprehend the surprise?" Ugo Corte glanced up from the maps and papers spread along the grass to question Carlo ironically, while the latter appeared to be keeping rigid watch over the safety of the position. Carlo puffed the smoke of a cigarette rapidly, and Agostino replied for him:—

"From the quarter where the best donkeys are to be had."

It was supposed that Agostino had resumed the habit usually laid aside by him for the discussion of serious matters, and had condescended to father a coarse joke; but his eyes showed no spark of their well-known twinkling solicitation for laughter, and Carlo spoke in answer gravely:—

"From Baveno it will be."

"From Baveno! They might as well think to surprise hawks from Baveno.
Keep watch, dear Ammiani; a good start in a race is a kick from the Gods."

With that, Corte turned to the point of his finger on the map. He conceived it possible that Carlo Ammiani, a Milanese, had reason to anticipate the approach of people by whom he, or they, might not wish to be seen. Had he studied Carlo's face he would have been reassured. The brows of the youth were open, and his eyes eager with expectation, that showed the flying forward of the mind, and nothing of knotted distrust or wary watchfulness. Now and then he would move to the other side of the mountain, and look over upon Orta; or with the opera-glass clasped in one hand beneath an arm, he stopped in his sentinel-march, frowning reflectively at a word put to him, as if debating within upon all the bearings of it; but the only answer that came was a sharp assent, given after the manner of one who dealt conscientiously in definite affirmatives; and again the glass was in requisition. Marco Sana was a fighting soldier, who stated what he knew, listened, and took his orders. Giulio Bandinelli was also little better than the lieutenant in an enterprise. Corte, on the other hand, had the conspirator's head,—a head like a walnut, bulging above the ears,—and the man was of a sallying temper. He lay there putting bit by bit of his plot before the Chief for his approval, with a careful construction, that upon the expression of any doubt of its working smoothly in the streets of Milan, caused him to shout a defensive, "But Carlo says yes!"

This uniform character of Ammiani's replies, and the smile of Agostino on hearing them, had begun to strike the attention of the soldierly Marco Sana. He ran his hand across his shorn head, and puffed his burnt red mole-spotted cheeks, with a sidelong stare at the abstracted youth, "Said yes!" he remarked. "He might say no, for a diversion. He has yeses enough in his pay to earn a Cardinal's hat. 'Is Milan preparing to rise?' 'Yes.'—'Is she ready for the work?' 'Yes.'—'Is the garrison on its guard?' 'Yes.'—'Have you seen Barto Rizzo?' 'Yes.'—'Have the people got the last batch of arms?' 'Yes.'—And 'Yes,' the secret is well kept; 'Yes,' Barto Rizzo is steadily getting them together. We may rely on him: Carlo is his intimate friend: Yes, Yes:—There's a regiment of them at your service, and you may shuffle them as you will. This is the help we get from Milan: a specimen of what we may expect!"

Sana had puffed himself hot, and now blew for coolness.

"You are,"—Agostino addressed him,—"philosophically totally wrong, my Marco. Those affirmatives are fat worms for the catching of fish. They are the real pretty fruit of the Hesperides. Personally, you or I may be irritated by them: but I'm not sure they don't please us. Were Carlo a woman, of course he should learn to say no;—as he will now if I ask him, Is she in sight? I won't do it, you know; but as a man and a diplomatist, it strikes me that he can't say yes too often."

"Answer me, Count Ammiani, and do me the favour to attend to these trifles for the space of two minutes," said Corte. "Have you seen Barto Rizzo? Is he acting for Medole?"

"As mole, as reindeer, and as bloody northern Raven!" ejaculated Agostino: "perhaps to be jackal, by-and-by. But I do not care to abuse our Barto Rizzo, who is a prodigy of nature, and has, luckily for himself, embraced a good cause, for he is certain to be hanged if he is not shot. He has the prophetic owl's face. I have always a fancy of his hooting his own death-scrip. I wrong our Barto:—Medole would be the jackal, if it lay between the two."

Carlo Ammiani had corrected Corte's manner to him by a complacent readiness to give him distinct replies. He then turned and set off at full speed down the mountain.

"She is sighted at last," Agostino murmured, and added rapidly some spirited words under his breath to the Chief, whose chin was resting on his doubled hand.

Corte, Marco, and Giulio were full of denunciations against Milan and the Milanese, who had sent a boy to their councils. It was Brescia and Bergamo speaking in their jealousy, but Carlo's behaviour was odd, and called for reproof. He had come as the deputy of Milan to meet the Chief, and he had not spoken a serious word on the great business of the hour, though the plot had been unfolded, the numbers sworn to, and Brescia, and Bergamo, and Cremona, and Venice had spoken upon all points through their emissaries, the two latter cities being represented by Sana and Corte.

"We've had enough of this lad," said Corte. "His laundress is following him with a change of linen, I suppose, or it's a scent-bottle. He's an admirable representative of the Lombard metropolis!" Corte drawled out the words in prodigious mimicry. "If Milan has nothing better to send than such a fellow, we'll finish without her, and shame the beast that she is. She has been always a treacherous beast!"

"Poor Milan!" sighed the Chief; "she lies under the beak of the vulture, and has twice been devoured; but she has a soul: she proves it. Ammiani, too, will prove his value. I have no doubt of him. As to boys, or even girls, you know my faith is in the young. Through them Italy lives. What power can teach devotion to the old?"

"I thank you, signore," Agostino gesticulated.

"But, tell me, when did you learn it, my friend?"

In answer, Agostino lifted his hand a little boy's height from the earth.

The old man then said: "I am afraid, my dear Corte, you must accept the fellowship of a girl as well as of a boy upon this occasion. See! our Carlo! You recognize that dancing speck below there?—he has joined himself—the poor lad wishes he could, I dare swear!—to another bigger speck, which is verily a lady: who has joined herself to a donkey—a common habit of the sex, I am told; but I know them not. That lady, signor Ugo, is the signorina Vittoria. You stare? But, I tell you, the game cannot go on without her; and that is why I have permitted you to knock the ball about at your own pleasure for these forty minutes."

Corte drew his under-lip on his reddish stubble moustache. "Are we to have women in a conference?" he asked from eye to eye.

"Keep to the number, Ugo; and moreover, she is not a woman, but a noble virgin. I discern a distinction, though you may not. The Vestal's fire burns straight."

"Who is she?"

"It rejoices me that she should be so little known. All the greater the illumination when her light shines out! The signorina Vittoria is a cantatrice who is about to appear upon the boards."

"Ah! that completes it." Corte rose to his feet with an air of desperation. "We require to be refreshed with quavers and crescendos and trillets! Who ever knew a singer that cared an inch of flesh for her country? Money, flowers, flattery, vivas! but, money! money! and Austrian as good as Italian. I've seen the accursed wenches bow gratefully for Austrian bouquets:—bow? ay, and more; and when the Austrian came to them red with our blood. I spit upon their polluted cheeks! They get us an ill name wherever they go. These singers have no country. One—I knew her—betrayed Filippo Mastalone, and sang the night of the day he was shot. I heard the white demon myself. I could have taken her long neck till she twisted like a serpent and hissed. May heaven forgive me for not levelling a pistol at her head! If God, my friends, had put the thought into my brain that night!"

A flush had deadened Corte's face to the hue of nightshade.

"You thunder in a clear atmosphere, my Ugo," returned the old man, as he fell back calmly at full length.

"And who is this signorina Vittoria?" cried Corte.

"A cantatrice who is about to appear upon the boards, as I have already remarked: of La Scala, let me add, if you hold it necessary."

"And what does she do here?"

"Her object in coming, my friend? Her object in coming is, first, to make her reverence to one who happens to be among us this day; and secondly, but principally, to submit a proposition to him and to us."

"What's her age?" Corte sneered.

"According to what calendar would you have it reckoned? Wisdom would say sixty: Father Chronos might divide that by three, and would get scarce a month in addition, hungry as he is for her, and all of us! But Minerva's handmaiden has no age. And now, dear Ugo, you have your opportunity to denounce her as a convicted screecher by night. Do so."

Corte turned his face to the Chief, and they spoke together for some minutes: after which, having had names of noble devoted women, dead and living, cited to him, in answer to brutal bellowings against that sex, and hearing of the damsel under debate as one who was expected and was welcome, he flung himself upon the ground again, inviting calamity by premature resignation. Giulio Bandinelli stretched his hand for Carlo's glass, and spied the approach of the signorina.

"Dark," he said.

"A jewel of that complexion," added Agostino, by way of comment.

"She has scorching eyes."

"She may do mischief; she may do mischief; let it be only on the right Side!"

"She looks fat."

"She sits doubled up and forward, don't you see, to relieve the poor donkey. You, my Giulio, would call a swan fat if the neck were not always on the stretch."

"By Bacchus! what a throat she has!"

"And well interjected, Giulio! It runs down like wine, like wine, to the little ebbing and flowing wave! Away with the glass, my boy! You must trust to all that's best about you to spy what's within. She makes me young—young!"

Agostino waved his hand in the form of a salute to her on the last short ascent. She acknowledged it gracefully; and talking at intervals to Carlo Ammiani, who footed briskly by her side, she drew by degrees among the eyes fixed on her, some of which were not gentle; but hers were for the Chief, at whose feet, when dismounted by Ammiani's solicitous aid, she would have knelt, had he not seized her by her elbows, and put his lips to her cheek.

"The signorina Vittoria, gentlemen," said Agostino.

CHAPTER III
SIGNORINA VITTORIA

The old man had introduced her with much of the pride of a father displaying some noble child of his for the first time to admiring friends.

"She is one of us," he pursued; "a daughter of Italy! My daughter also; is it not so?"

He turned to her as for a confirmation. The signorina pressed his fingers. She was a little intimidated, and for the moment seemed shy and girlish. The shade of her broad straw hat partly concealed her vivid features.

"Now, gentlemen, if you please, the number is complete, and we may proceed to business," said Agostino, formally but as he conducted the signorina to place her at the feet of the Chief, she beckoned to her servant, who was holding the animal she had ridden. He came up to her, and presented himself in something of a military posture of attention to her commands. These were that he should take the poor brute to water, and then lead him back to Baveno, and do duty in waiting upon her mother. The first injunction was received in a decidedly acquiescent manner. On hearing the second, which directed his abandonment of his post of immediate watchfulness over her safety, the man flatly objected with a "Signorina, no."

He was a handsome bright-eyed fellow, with a soldier's frame and a smile as broad and beaming as laughter, indicating much of that mixture of acuteness, and simplicity which is a characteristic of the South, and means no more than that the extreme vivacity of the blood exceeds at times that of the brain.

A curious frown of half-amused astonishment hung on the signorina's face.

"When I tell you to go, Beppo!"

At once the man threw out his fingers, accompanied by an amazingly voluble delivery of his reasons for this revolt against her authority. Among other things, he spoke of an oath sworn by him to a foreign gentleman, his patron,—for whom, and for whomsoever he loved, he was ready to pour forth his heart's blood,—to the effect that he would never quit her side when she left the roof of her house.

"You see, Beppo," she remonstrated, "I am among friends."

Beppo gave a sweeping bow, but remained firm where he stood. Ammiani cast a sharp hard look at the man.

"Do you hear the signorina's orders?"

"I hear them, signore."

"Will you obey them?"

She interposed. "He must not hear quick words. Beppo is only showing his love for his master and for me. But you are wrong in this case, my Beppo. You shall give me your protection when I require it; and now, you are sensible, and must understand that it is not wanted. I tell you to go."

Beppo read the eyes of his young mistress.

"Signorina,"—he stooped forward mysteriously,—"signorina, that fellow is in Baveno. I saw him this morning."

"Good, good. And now go, my friend."

"The signor Agostino," he remarked loudly, to attract the old man; "the signor Agostino may think proper to advise you."

"The signor Agostino will laugh at nothing that you say to-day, Beppo. You will obey me. Go at once," she repeated, seeing him on tiptoe to gain Agostino's attention.

Beppo knew by her eyes that her ears were locked against him; and, though she spoke softly, there was an imperiousness in her voice not to be disregarded. He showed plainly by the lost rigidity of his attitude that he was beaten and perplexed. Further expostulations being disregarded, he turned his head to look at the poor panting beast under his charge, and went slowly up to him: they walked off together, a crest-fallen pair.

"You have gained the victory, signorina," said Ugo Corte.

She replied, smiling, "My poor Beppo! it's not difficult to get the best of those who love us."

"Ha!" cried Agostino; "here is one of their secrets, Carlo. Take heed of it, my boy. We shall have queens when kings are fossils, mark me!"

Ammiani muttered a courtly phrase, whereat Corte yawned in very grim fashion.

The signorina had dropped to the grass, at a short step from the Chief, to whom her face was now seriously given. In Ammiani's sight she looked a dark Madonna, with the sun shining bright gold through the edges of the summer hat, thrown back from her head. The full and steady contemplative eyes had taken their fixed expression, after a vanishing affectionate gaze of an instant cast upon Agostino. Attentive as they were, light played in them like water. The countenance was vivid in repose. She leaned slightly forward, clasping the wrist of one hand about her knee, and the sole of one little foot showed from under her dress.

Deliberately, but with no attempt at dramatic impressiveness, the Chief began to speak. He touched upon the condition of Italy, and the new lilt animating her young men and women. "I have heard many good men jeer," he said, "at our taking women to our counsel, accepting their help, and putting a great stake upon their devotion. You have read history, and you know what women can accomplish. They may be trained, equally as we are, to venerate the abstract idea of country, and be a sacrifice to it. Without their aid, and the fire of a fresh life being kindled in their bosoms, no country that has lain like ours in the death-trance can revive. In the death-trance, I say, for Italy does not die!"

"True," said other voices.

"We have this belief in the eternal life of our country, and the belief is the life itself. But let no strong man among us despise the help of women. I have seen our cause lie desperate, and those who despaired of it were not women. Women kept the flame alive. They worship in the temple of the cause."

Ammiani's eyes dwelt fervidly upon the signorina. Her look, which was fastened upon the Chief, expressed a mind that listened to strange matter concerning her very little. But when the plans for the rising of the Bergamascs and Brescians, the Venetians, the Bolognese, the Milanese, all the principal Northern cities, were recited, with a practical emphasis thrown upon numbers, upon the readiness of the organized bands, the dispositions of the leaders, and the amount of resistance to be expected at the various points indicated for the outbreak, her hands disjoined, and she stretched her fingers to the grass, supporting herself so, while her extended chin and animated features told how eagerly her spirit drank at positive springs, and thirsted for assurance of the coming storm.

"It is decided that Milan gives the signal," said the Chief; and a light, like the reflection of a beacon-fire upon the night, flashed over her.

He was pursuing, when Ugo Corte smote the air with his nervous fingers, crying out passionately, "Bunglers! are we again to wait for them, and hear that fifteen patriots have stabbed a Croat corporal, and wrestled hotly with a lieutenant of the guard? I say they are bunglers. They never mean the thing. Fifteen! There were just three Milanese among the last lot—the pick of the city; and the rest were made up of Trentini, and our lads from Bergamo and Brescia; and the order from the Council was, 'Go and do the business!' which means, 'Go and earn your ounce of Austrian lead.' They went, and we gave fifteen true men for one poor devil of a curst tight blue-leg. They can play the game on if we give them odds like that. Milan burns bad powder, and goes off like a drugged pistol. It's a nest of bunglers, and may it be razed! We could do without it, and well! If it were a family failing, should not I too be trusting them? My brother was one of the fifteen who marched out as targets to try the skill of those hell-plumed Tyrolese: and they did it thoroughly—shot him straight here." Corte struck his chest. "He gave a jump and a cry. Was it a viva for Milan? They swear that it was, and they can't translate from a living mouth, much more from a dead one; but I know my Niccolo better. I have kissed his lips a thousand times, and I know the poor boy meant, 'Scorn and eternal distrust of such peddling conspirators as these!' I can deal with traitors, but these flash-in- the-pan plotters—these shaking, jelly-bodied patriots!—trust to them again? Rather draw lots for another fifteen to bare their breasts and bandage their eyes, and march out in the grey morning, while the stupid Croat corporal goes on smoking his lumpy pipe! We shall hear that Milan is moving; we shall rise; we shall be hot at it; and the news will come that Milan has merely yawned and turned over to sleep on the other side. Twice she has done this trick, and the garrison there has sent five regiments to finish us—teach us to sleep soundly likewise! I say, let it be Bergamo; or be it Brescia, if you like; or Venice: she is ready. You trust to Milan, and you are fore-doomed. I would swear it with this hand in the flames. She give the signal? Shut your eyes, cross your hands flat on your breasts: you are dead men if you move. She lead the way? Spin on your heels, and you have followed her!"

Corte had spoken in a thick difficult voice, that seemed to require the aid of his vehement gestures to pour out as it did like a water-pipe in a hurricane of rain. He ceased, red almost to blackness, and knotted his arms, that were big as the cable of a vessel. Not a murmur followed his speech. The word was, given to the Chief, and he resumed:—

"You have a personal feeling in this case, Ugo. You have not heard me. I came through Paris. A rocket will soon shoot up from Paris that will be a signal for Christendom. The keen French wit is sick of its compromise-king. All Europe is in convulsions in a few months: to-morrow it may be. The elements are in the hearts of the people, and nothing will contain them. We have sown them to reap them. The sowing asks for persistency; but the reaping demands skill and absolute truthfulness. We have now one of those occasions coming which are the flowers to be plucked by resolute and worthy hands: they are the tests of our sincerity. This time now rapidly approaching will try us all, and we must be ready for it. If we have believed in it, we stand prepared. If we have conceived our plan of action in purity of heart, we shall be guided to discern the means which may serve us. You will know speedily what it is that has prompted you to move. If passion blindfolds you, if you are foiled by a prejudice, I also shall know. My friend, the nursing of a single antipathy is a presumption that your motive force is personal—whether the thirst for vengeance or some internal union of a hundred indistinct little fits of egoism. I have seen brave and even noble men fail at the ordeal of such an hour: not fail in courage, not fail in the strength of their desire; that was the misery for them! They failed because midway they lost the vision to select the right instruments put in our way by heaven. That vision belongs solely to such as have clean and disciplined hearts. The hope in the bosom of a man whose fixed star is Humanity becomes a part of his blood, and is extinguished when his blood flows no more. To conquer him, the principle of life must be conquered. And he, my friend, will use all, because he serves all. I need not touch on Milan."

The signorina drew in her breath quickly, as if in this abrupt close she had a revelation of the Chief's whole meaning, and was startled by the sudden unveiling of his mastery. Her hands hung loose; her figure was tremulous. A murmur from Corte jarred within her like a furious discord, but he had not offended by refusing to disclaim his error, and had simply said in a gruff acquiescent way, "Proceed." Her sensations of surprise at the singular triumph of the Chief made her look curiously into the faces of the other men; but the pronouncing of her name engaged her attention.

"Your first night is the night of the fifteenth of next month?"

"It is, signore," she replied, abashed to find herself speaking with him who had so moved her.

"There is no likelihood of a postponement?"

"I am certain, signore, that I shall be ready."

"There are no squabbles of any serious kind among the singers?"

A soft dimple played for a moment on her lips. "I have heard something."

"Among the women?"

"Yes, and the men."

"But the men do not concern you?"

"No, signore. Except that the women twist them."

Agostino chuckled audibly. The Chief resumed:

"You believe, notwithstanding, that all will go well? The opera will be acted; and you will appear in it?"

"Yes, signore. I know one who has determined on it, and can do it."

"Good. The opera is Camilla?"

She was answering with an affirmative, when Agostino broke in,—

"Camilla! And honour to whom honour is due! Let Caesar claim the writing of the libretto, if it be Caesar's! It has passed the censorship, signed Agostino Balderini—a disaffected person out of Piedmont, rendered tame and fangless by a rigorous imprisonment. The sources of the tale, O ye grave Signori Tedeschi? The sources are partly to be traced to a neat little French vaudeville, very sparkling—Camille, or the Husband Asserted; and again to a certain Chronicle that may be mediaeval, may be modern, and is just, as the great Shakespeare would say, 'as you like it.'"

Agostino recited some mock verses, burlesquing the ordinary libretti, and provoked loud laughter from Carlo Ammiani, who was familiar enough with the run of their nonsense.

"Camilla is the bride of Camillo. I give to her all the brains, which is a modern idea, quite! He does all the mischief, which is possibly mediaeval. They have both an enemy, which is mediaeval and modern. None of them know exactly what they are about; so there you have the modern, the mediaeval, and the antique, all in one. Finally, my friends, Camilla is something for you to digest at leisure. The censorship swallowed it at a gulp. Never was bait so handsomely taken! At present I have the joy of playing my fish. On the night of the fifteenth I land him. Camilla has a mother. Do you see? That mother is reported, is generally conceived, as dead. Do you see further? Camilla's first song treats of a dream she has had of that mother. Our signorina shall not be troubled to favour you with a taste of it, or, by Bacchus and his Indian nymphs, I should speedily behold you jumping like peas in a pan, like trout on a bank! The earth would be hot under you, verily! As I was remarking, or meant to be, Camilla and her husband disagree, having agreed to. 'Tis a plot to deceive Count Orso—aha? You are acquainted with Count Orso! He is Camilla's antenuptial guardian. Now you warm to it! In that condition I leave you. Perhaps my child here will give you a taste of her voice. The poetry does much upon reflection, but it has to ripen within you—a matter of time. Wed this voice to the poetry, and it finds passage 'twixt your ribs, as on the point of a driven blade. Do I cry the sweetness and the coolness of my melons? Not I! Try them."

The signorina put her hand out for the scroll he was unfolding, and cast her eyes along bars of music, while Agostino called a "Silenzio tutti!" She sang one verse, and stopped for breath.

Between her dismayed breathings she said to the Chief:—

"Believe me, signore, I can be trusted to sing when the time comes."

"Sing on, my blackbird—my viola!" said Agostino. "We all trust you. Look at Colonel Corte, and take him for Count Orso. Take me for pretty Camillo. Take Marco for Michiela; Giulio for Leonardo; Carlo for Cupid. Take the Chief for the audience. Take him for a frivolous public. Ah, my Pippo!" (Agostino laughed aside to him). "Let us lead off with a lighter piece; a trifle-tra-la-la! and then let the frisky piccolo be drowned in deep organ notes, as on some occasions in history the people overrun certain puling characters. But that, I confess, is an illustration altogether out of place, and I'll simply jot it down in my notebook."

Agostino had talked on to let her gain confidence. When he was silent she sang from memory. It was a song of flourishes: one of those be- flowered arias in which the notes flicker and leap like young flames. Others might have sung it; and though it spoke favourably of her aptitude and musical education, and was of a quality to enrapture easy, merely critical audiences, it won no applause from these men. The effect produced by it was exhibited in the placid tolerance shown by the uplifting of Ugo Corte's eyebrows, which said, "Well, here's a voice, certainly." His subsequent look added, "Is this what we have come hither to hear?"

Vittoria saw the look. "Am I on my trial before you?" she thought; and the thought nerved her throat. She sang in strong and grave contralto tones, at first with shut eyes. The sense of hostility left her, and left her soul free, and she raised them. The song was of Camilla dying. She pardons the treacherous hand, commending her memory and the strength of her faith to her husband:—

"Beloved, I am quickly out of sight:
I pray that you will love more than my dust.

Were death defeat, much weeping would be right;
'Tis victory when it leaves surviving trust.
You will not find me save when you forget
Earth's feebleness, and come to faith, my friend,
For all Humanity doth owe a debt
To all Humanity, until the end."

Agostino glanced at the Chief to see whether his ear had caught note of his own language.

The melancholy severity of that song of death changed to a song of prophetic triumph. The signorina stood up. Camilla has thrown off the mask, and has sung the name "Italia!" At the recurrence of it the men rose likewise.

"Italia, Italia, shall be free!"

Vittoria gave the inspiration of a dying voice: the conquest of death by an eternal truth seemed to radiate from her. Voice and features were as one expression of a rapture of belief built upon pathetic trustfulness.

"Italia, Italia shall be free!"

She seized the hearts of those hard and serious men as a wind takes the strong oak-trees, and rocks them on their knotted roots, and leaves them with the song of soaring among their branches. Italy shone about her; the lake, the plains, the peaks, and the shouldering flushed snowridges. Carlo Ammiani breathed as one who draws in fire. Grizzled Agostino glittered with suppressed emotion, like a frosted thorn-bush in the sunlight. Ugo Corte had his thick brows down, as a man who is reading iron matter. The Chief alone showed no sign beyond a half lifting of the hand, and a most luminous fixed observation of the fair young woman, from whom power was an emanation, free of effort. The gaze was sad in its thoughtfulness, such as our feelings translate of the light of evening.

She ceased, and he said, "You sing on the night of the fifteenth?"

"I do, signore."

"It is your first appearance?"

She bent her head.

"And you will be prepared on that night to sing this song?"

"Yes, signore."

"Save in the event of your being forbidden?"

"Unless you shall forbid me, I will sing it, signore."

"Should they imprison you?—"

"If they shoot me I shall be satisfied to know that I have sung a song that cannot be forgotten."

The Chief took her hand in a gentle grasp.

"Such as you will help to give our Italy freedom. You hold the sacred flame, and know you hold it in trust."

"Friends,"—he turned to his companions,—"you have heard what will be the signal for Milan."

CHAPTER IV
AMMIANI'S INTERCESSION

It was a surprise to all of them, save to Agostino Balderini, who passed his inspecting glance from face to face, marking the effect of the announcement. Corte gazed at her heavily, but not altogether disapprovingly. Giulio Bandinelli and Marco Sana, though evidently astonished, and to some extent incredulous, listened like the perfectly trusty lieutenants in an enterprise which they were. But Carlo Ammiani stood horror-stricken. The blood had left his handsome young olive-hued face, and his eyes were on the signorina, large with amazement, from which they deepened to piteousness of entreaty.

"Signorina!—you! Can it be true? Do you know?—do you mean it?"

"What, signor Carlo?"

"This; will you venture to do such a thing?"

"Oh, will I venture? What can you think of me? It is my own request."

"But, signorina, in mercy, listen and consider."

Carlo turned impetuously to the Chief. "The signorina can't know the danger she is running. She will be seized on the boards, and shut up between four walls before a man of us will be ready,—or more than one," he added softly. "The house is sure to be packed for a first night; and the Polizia have a suspicion of her. She has been off her guard in the Conservatorio; she has talked of a country called Italy; she has been indiscreet;—pardon, pardon, signorina! but it is true that she has spoken out from her noble heart. And this opera! Are they fools?—they must see through it. It will never,—it can't possibly be reckoned on to appear. I knew that the signorina was heart and soul with us; but who could guess that her object was to sacrifice herself in the front rank,— to lead a forlorn hope! I tell you it's like a Pagan rite. You are positively slaying a victim. I beg you all to look at the case calmly!"

A burst of laughter checked him; for his seniors by many years could not hear such veteran's counsel from a hurried boy without being shrewdly touched by the humour of it, while one or two threw a particular irony into their tones.

"When we do slay a victim, we will come to you as our augur, my Carlo," said Agostino.

Corte was less gentle. As a Milanese and a mere youth Ammiani was antipathetic to Corte, who closed his laughter with a windy rattle of his lips, and a "pish!" of some emphasis.

Carlo was quick to give him a challenging frown.

"What is it?" Corte bent his head back, as if inquiringly.

"It's I who claim that question by right," said Carlo.

"You are a boy."

"I have studied war."

"In books."

"With brains, Colonel Corte."

"War is a matter of blows, my little lad."

"Let me inform you, signor Colonel, that war is not a game between bulls, to be played with the horns of the head."

"You are prepared to instruct me?" The fiery Bergamasc lifted his eyebrows.

"Nay, nay!" said Agostino. "Between us two first;" and he grasped Carlo's arm, saying in an underbreath, "Your last retort was too long- winded. In these conflicts you must be quick, sharp as a rifle-crack that hits echo on the breast-bone and makes her cry out. I correct a student in the art of war." Then aloud: "My opera, young man!—well, it's my libretto, and you know we writers always say 'my opera' when we have put the pegs for the voice; you are certainly aware that we do. How dare you to make calumnious observations upon my opera? Is it not the ripe and admirable fruit of five years of confinement? Are not the lines sharp, the stanzas solid? and the stuff, is it not good? Is not the subject simple, pure from offence to sensitive authority, constitutionally harmless? Reply!"

"It's transparent to any but asses," said Carlo.

"But if it has passed the censorship? You are guilty, my boy, of bestowing upon those highly disciplined gentlemen who govern your famous city—what title? I trust a prophetic one, since that it comes from an animal whose custom is to turn its back before it delivers a blow, and is, they remark, fonder of encountering dead lions than live ones. Still, it is you who are indiscreet,—eminently so, I must add, if you will look lofty. If my opera has passed the censorship! eh, what have you to say?"

Carlo endured this banter till the end of it came.

"And you—you encourage her!" he cried wrathfully. "You know what the danger is for her, if they once lay hands on her. They will have her in Verona in four-and-twenty hours; through the gates of the Adige in a couple of days, and at Spielberg, or some other of their infernal dens of groans, within a week. Where is the chance of a rescue then? They torture, too, they torture! It's a woman; and insult will be one mode of torturing her. They can use rods—"

The excited Southern youth was about to cover his face, but caught back his hands, clenching them.

"All this," said Agostino, "is an evasion, manifestly, of the question concerning my opera, on which you have thought proper to cast a slur. The phrase, 'transparent to any but asses,' may not be absolutely objectionable, for transparency is, as the critics rightly insist, meritorious in a composition. And, according to the other view, if we desire our clever opponents to see nothing in something, it is notably skilful to let them see through it. You perceive, my Carlo. Transparency, then, deserves favourable comment. So, I do not complain of your phrase, but I had the unfortunate privilege of hearing it uttered. The method of delivery scarcely conveyed a compliment. Will you apologize?"

Carlo burst from him with a vehement question to the Chief: "Is it decided?"

"It is, my friend," was the reply.

"Decided! She is doomed! Signorina! what can you know of this frightful risk? You are going to the slaughter. You will be seized before the first verse is out of your lips, and once in their clutches, you will never breathe free air again. It's madness!—ah, forgive me!—yes, madness! For you shut your eyes; you rush into the trap blindfolded. And that is how you serve our Italy! She sees you an instant, and you are caught away;—and you who might serve her, if you would, do you think you can move dungeon walls?"

"Perhaps, if I have been once seen, I shall not be forgotten," said the signorina smoothly, and then cast her eyes down, as if she felt the burden of a little possible accusation of vanity in this remark. She raised them with fire.

"No; never!" exclaimed Carlo. "But, now you are ours. And—surely it is not quite decided?"

He had spoken imploringly to the Chief. "Not irrevocably?" he added.

"Irrevocably!"

"Then she is lost!"

"For shame, Carlo Ammiani;" said old Agostino, casting his sententious humours aside. "Do you not hear? It is decided! Do you wish to rob her of her courage, and see her tremble? It's her scheme and mine: a case where an old head approves a young one. The Chief says Yes! and you bellow still! Is it a Milanese trick? Be silent."

"Be silent!" echoed Carlo. "Do you remember the beast Marschatska's bet?" The allusion was to a black incident concerning a young Italian ballet girl who had been carried off by an Austrian officer, under the pretext of her complicity in one of the antecedent conspiracies.

"He rendered payment for it," said Agostino.

"He perished; yes! as we shake dust to the winds; but she!—it's terrible! You place women in the front ranks—girls! What can defenceless creatures do? Would you let the van-regiment in battle be the one without weapons? It's slaughter. She's like a lamb to them. You hold up your jewel to the enemy, and cry, 'Come and take it.' Think of the insults! think of the rough hands, and foul mouths! She will be seized on the boards—"

"Not if you keep your tongue from wagging," interposed Ugo Corte, fevered by this unseasonable exhibition of what was to him manifestly a lover's frenzied selfishness. He moved off, indifferent to Carlo's retort. Marco Sana and Giulio Bandinelli were already talking aside with the Chief.

"Signor Carlo, not a hand shall touch me," said the signorina. "And I am not a lamb, though it is good of you to think me one. I passed through the streets of Milan in the last rising. I was unharmed. You must have some confidence in me."

"Signorina, there's the danger," rejoined Carlo. "You trust to your good angels once, twice—the third time they fail you! What are you among a host of armed savages? You would be tossed like weed on the sea. In pity, do not look so scornfully! No, there is no unjust meaning in it; but you despise me for seeing danger. Can nothing persuade you? And, besides," he addressed the Chief, who alone betrayed no signs of weariness; "listen, I beg of you. Milan wants no more than a signal. She does not require to be excited. I came charged with several proposals for giving the alarm. Attend, you others! The night of the Fifteenth comes; it is passing like an ordinary night. At twelve a fire- balloon is seen in the sky. Listen, in the name of saints and devils!"

But even the Chief was observed to show signs of amusement, and the gravity of the rest forsook them altogether at the display of this profound and original conspiratorial notion.

"Excellent! excellent! my Carlo," said old Agostino, cheerfully. "You have thought. You must have thought, or whence such a conception? But, you really mistake. It is not the garrison whom we desire to put on their guard. By no means. We are not in the Imperial pay. Probably your balloon is to burst in due time, and, wind permitting, disperse printed papers all over the city?"

"What if it is?" cried Carlo fiercely.

"Exactly. I have divined your idea. You have thought, or, to correct the tense, are thinking, which is more hopeful, though it may chance not to seem so meritorious. But, if yours are the ideas of full-blown jackets, bear in mind that our enemies are coated and breeched. It may be creditable to you that your cunning is not the cunning of the serpent; to us it would be more valuable if it were. Continue."

"Oh! there are a thousand ways." Carlo controlled himself with a sharp screw of all his muscles. "I simply wish to save the signorina from an annoyance."

"Very mildly put," Agostino murmured assentingly.

"In our Journal," said Carlo, holding out the palm of one hand to dot the forefinger of the other across it, by way of personal illustration—"in our Journal we might arrange for certain letters to recur at distinct intervals in Roman capitals, which might spell out, 'This Night AT Twelve,' or 'At Once.'"

"Quite as ingenious, but on the present occasion erring on the side of intricacy. Aha! you want to increase the sale of your Journal, do you, my boy? The rogue!"

With which, and a light slap over Carlo's shoulder, Agostino left him.

The aspect of his own futile proposals stared the young man in the face too forcibly for him to nurse the spark of resentment which was struck out in the turmoil of his bosom. He veered, as if to follow Agostino, and remained midway, his chest heaving, and his eyelids shut.

"Signor Carlo, I have not thanked you." He heard Vittoria speak. "I know that a woman should never attempt to do men's work. The Chief will tell you that we must all serve now, and all do our best. If we fail, and they put me to great indignity, I promise you that I will not live. I would give this up to be done by anyone else who could do it better. It is in my hands, and my friends must encourage me."

"Ah, signorina!" the young man sighed bitterly. The knowledge that he had already betrayed himself in the presence of others too far, and the sob in his throat labouring to escape, kept him still.

A warning call from Ugo Corte drew their attention. Close by the chalet where the first climbers of the mountain had refreshed themselves, Beppo was seen struggling to secure the arms of a man in a high-crowned green Swiss hat, who was apparently disposed to give the signorina's faithful servant some trouble. After gazing a minute at this singular contention, she cried—

"It's the same who follows me everywhere!"

"And you will not believe you are suspected," murmured Carlo in her ear.

"A spy?" Sana queried, showing keen joy at the prospect of scotching such a reptile on the lonely height. Corte went up to the Chief. They spoke briefly together, making use of notes and tracings on paper. The Chief then said "Adieu" to the signorina. It was explained to the rest by Corte that he had a meeting to attend near Pella about noon, and must be in Fobello before midnight. Thence his way would be to Genoa.

"So, you are resolved to give another trial to our crowned ex-Carbonaro," said Agostino.

"Without leaving him an initiative this time!" and the Chief embraced the old man. "You know me upon that point. I cannot trust him. I do not. But, if we make such a tide in Lombardy that his army must be drawn into it, is such an army to be refused? First, the tide, my friend! See to that."

"The king is our instrument!" cried Carlo Ammiani, brightening.

"Yes, if we were particularly well skilled in the use of that kind of instrument," Agostino muttered.

He stood apart while the Chief said a few words to Carlo, which made the blood play vividly across the visage of the youth. Carlo tried humbly to expostulate once or twice. In the end his head was bowed, and he signified a dumb acquiescence.

"Once more, good-bye." The Chief addressed the signorina in English.

She replied in the same tongue, "Good-bye," tremulously; and passion mounting on it, added—"Oh! when shall I see you again?"

"When Rome is purified to be a fit place for such as you."

In another minute he was hidden on the slope of the mountain lying toward Orta.

CHAPTER V
THE SPY

Beppo had effected a firm capture of his man some way down the slope. But it was a case of check that entirely precluded his own free movements. They hung together intertwisted in the characters of specious pacificator and appealing citizen, both breathless.

"There! you want to hand me up neatly; I know your vanity, my Beppo; and you don't even know my name," said the prisoner.

"I know your ferret of a face well enough," said Beppo. "You dog the signorina. Come up, and don't give trouble."

"Am I not a sheep? You worry me. Let me go."

"You're a wriggling eel."

"Catch me fast by the tail then, and don't hold me by the middle."

"You want frightening, my pretty fellow!"

"If that's true, my Beppo, somebody made a mistake in sending you to do it. Stop a moment. You're blown. I think you gulp down your minestra too hot; you drink beer."

"You dog the signorina! I swore to scotch you at last."

"I left Milan for the purpose—don't you see? Act fairly, my Beppo, and let us go up to the signorina together decently."

"Ay, ay, my little reptile! You'll find no Austrians here. Cry out to them to come to you from Baveno. If the Motterone grew just one tree! Saints! one would serve."

"Why don't you—fool that you are, my Beppo!—pray to the saints earlier?
Trees don't grow from heaven."

"You'll be going there soon, and you'll know better about it."

"Thanks to the Virgin, then, we shall part at some time or other!"

The struggles between them continued sharply during this exchange of intellectual shots; but hearing Ugo Corte's voice, the prisoner's confident audacity forsook him, and he drew a long tight face like the mask of an admonitory exclamation addressed to himself from within.

"Stand up straight!" the soldier's command was uttered.

Even Beppo was amazed to see that the man had lost the power to obey or to speak.

Corte grasped him under the arm-pit. With the force of his huge fist he swung him round and stretched him out at arm's length, all collar and shanks. The man hung like a mole from the twig. Yet, while Beppo poured out the tale of his iniquities, his eyes gave the turn of a twinkle, showing that he could have answered one whom he did not fear. The charge brought against him was, that for the last six months he had been untiringly spying on the signorina.

Corte stamped his loose feet to earth, shook him and told him to walk aloft. The flexible voluble fellow had evidently become miserably disconcerted. He walked in trepidation, speechless, and when interrogated on the height his eyes flew across the angry visages with dismal uncertainty. Agostino perceived that he had undoubtedly not expected to come among them, and forthwith began to excite Giulio and Marco to the worst suspicions, in order to indulge his royal poetic soul with a study of a timorous wretch pushed to anticipations of extremity.

"The execution of a spy," he preluded, "is the signal for the ringing of joy-bells on this earth; not only because he is one of a pestiferous excess, in point of numbers, but that he is no true son of earth. He escaped out of hell's doors on a windy day, and all that we do is to puff out a bad light, and send him back. Look at this fellow in whom conscience is operating so that he appears like a corked volcano! You can see that he takes Austrian money; his skin has got to be the exact colour of Munz. He has the greenish-yellow eyes of those elective, thrice-abhorred vampyres who feed on patriot-blood. He is condemned without trial by his villanous countenance, like an ungrammatical preface to a book. His tongue refuses to confess, but nature is stronger:— observe his knees. Now this is guilt. It is execrable guilt. He is a nasty object. Nature has in her wisdom shortened his stature to indicate that it is left to us to shorten the growth of his offending years. Now, you dangling soul! answer me:—what name hailed you when on earth?"

The fan, with no clearly serviceable tongue, articulated, "Luigi."

"Luigi! the name Christian and distinctive. The name historic:-Luigi Porco?"

"Luigi Saracco, signore."

"Saracco: Saracco: very possibly a strip of the posterity of cut-throat Moors. To judge by your face, a Moor undoubtedly: glib, slippery! with a body that slides and a soul that jumps. Taken altogether, more serpent than eagle. I misdoubt that little quick cornering eye of yours. Do you ever remember to have blushed?"

"No, signore," said Luigi.

"You spy upon the signorina, do you?"

"You have Beppo's word for that," interposed Marco Sana, growling.

"And you are found spying on the mountain this particular day! Luigi Saracco, you are a fellow of a tremendous composition. A goose walking into a den of foxes is alone to be compared to you,—if ever such goose was! How many of us did you count, now, when you were, say, a quarter of a mile below?"

Marco interposed again: "He has already seen enough up here to make a rope of florins."

"The fellow's eye takes likenesses," said Giulio.

Agostino's question was repeated by Corte, and so sternly that Luigi, beholding kindness upon no other face save Vittoria's, watched her, and muttering "Six," blinked his keen black eyes piteously to get her sign of assent to his hesitated naming of that number. Her mouth and the turn of her head were expressive to him, and he cried "Seven."

"So; first six, and next seven," said Corte.

"Six, I meant, without the signorina," Luigi explained.

"You saw six of us without the signorina! You see we are six here, including the signorina. Where is the seventh?"

Luigi tried to penetrate Vittoria's eyes for a proper response; but she understood the grave necessity for getting the full extent of his observations out of him, and she looked as remorseless as the men. He feigned stupidity and sullenness, rage and cunning, in quick succession.

"Who was the seventh?" said Carlo.

"Was it the king?" Luigi asked.

This was by just a little too clever; and its cleverness, being seen, magnified the intended evasion so as to make it appear to them that Luigi knew well the name of the seventh.

Marco thumped a hand on his shoulder, shouting—

"Here; speak out! You saw seven of us. Where has the seventh one gone?"

Luigi's wits made a dash at honesty. "Down Orta, signore."

"And down Orta, I think, you will go; deeper down than you may like."

Corte now requested Vittoria to stand aside. He motioned to her with his hand to stand farther, and still farther off; and finally told Carlo to escort her to Baveno. She now began to think that the man Luigi was in some perceptible danger, nor did Ammiani disperse the idea.

"If he is a spy, and if he has seen the Chief, we shall have to detain him for at least four-and-twenty hours," he said, "or do worse."

"But, Signor Carlo,"—Vittoria made appeal to his humanity,—"do they mean, if they decide that he is guilty, to hurt him?"

"Tell me, signorina, what punishment do you imagine a spy deserves?"

"To be called one!"

Carlo smiled at her lofty method of dealing with the animal.

"Then you presume him to have a conscience?"

"I am sure, Signor Carlo, that I could make him loathe to be called a spy."

They were slowly pacing from the group, and were on the edge of the descent, when the signorina's name was shrieked by Luigi. The man came running to her for protection, Beppo and the rest at his heels. She allowed him to grasp her hand.

"After all, he is my spy; he does belong to me," she said, still speaking on to Carlo. "I must beg your permission, Colonel Corte and Signor Marco, to try an experiment. The Signor Carlo will not believe that a spy can be ashamed of his name.—Luigi!"

"Signorina!"—he shook his body over her hand with a most plaintive utterance.

"You are my countryman, Luigi?"

"Yes, signorina."

"You are an Italian?"

"Certainly, signorina!"

"A spy!"

Vittoria had not always to lift her voice in music for it to sway the hearts of men. She spoke the word very simply in a mellow soft tone. Luigi's blood shot purple. He thrust his fists against his ears.

"See, Signor Carlo," she said; "I was right. Luigi, you will be a spy no more?"

Carlo Ammiani happened to be rolling a cigarette-paper. She put out her fingers for it, and then reached it to Luigi, who accepted it with singular contortions of his frame, declaring that he would confess everything to her. "Yes, signorina, it is true; I am a spy on you. I know the houses you visit. I know you eat too much chocolate for your voice. I know you are the friend of the Signora Laura, the widow of Giacomo Piaveni, shot—shot on Annunciation Day. The Virgin bless him! I know the turning of every street from your house near the Duomo to the signora's. You go nowhere else, except to the maestro's. And it's something to spy upon you. But think of your Beppo who spies upon me! And your little mother, the lady most excellent, is down in Baveno, and she is always near you when you make an expedition. Signorina, I know you would not pay your Beppo for spying upon me. Why does he do it? I do not sing 'Italia, Italia shall be free!' I have heard you when I was under the maestro's windows; and once you sang it to the Signor Agostino Balderini.

"Indeed, signorina, I am a sort of guardian of your voice. It is not gold of the Tedeschi I get from the Signor Antonio Pericles."

At the mention of this name, Agostino and Vittoria laughed out.

"You are in the pay of the Signor Antonio-Pericles," said Agostino.

"Without being in our pay, you have done us the service to come up here among us! Bravo! In return for your disinterestedness, we kick you down, either upon Baveno or upon Stresa, or across the lake, if you prefer it.—The man is harmless. He is hired by a particular worshipper of the signorina's voice, who affects to have first discovered it when she was in England, and is a connoisseur, a millionaire, a Greek, a rich scoundrel, with one indubitable passion, for which I praise him. We will let his paid eavesdropper depart, I think. He is harmless."

Neither Ugo nor Marco was disposed to allow any description of spy to escape unscotched. Vittoria saw that Luigi's looks were against him, and whispered: "Why do you show such cunning eyes, Luigi?"

He replied: "Signorina, take me out of their hearing, and I will tell you everything."

She walked aside. He seemed immediately to be inspired with confidence, and stretched his fingers in the form of a grasshopper, at which sight they cried: "He knows Barto Rizzo—this rascal!" They plied him with signs and countersigns, and speedily let him go. There ensued a sharp snapping of altercation between Luigi and Beppo. Vittoria had to order Beppo to stand back.

"It is a poor dog, not of a good breed, signorina," Luigi said, casting a tolerant glance over his shoulder. "Faithful, but a poor nose. Ah! you gave me this cigarette. Not the Virgin could have touched my marrow as you did. That's to be remembered by-and-by. Now, you are going to sing on the night of the fifteenth of September. Change that night. The Signor Antonio-Pericles watches you, and he is a friend of the Government, and the Government is snoring for you to think it asleep. The Signor Antonio-Pericles pacifies the Tedeschi, but he will know all that you are doing, and how easy it will be, and how simple, for you to let me know what you think he ought to know, and just enough to keep him comfortable! So we work like a machine, signorina. Only, not through that Beppo, for he is vain of his legs, and his looks, and his service, and because he has carried a gun and heard it go off. Yes; I am a spy. But I am honest. I, too, have visited England. One can be honest and a spy. Signorina, I have two arms, but only one heart. If you will be gracious and consider! Say, here are two hands. One hand does this thing, one hand does that thing, and that thing wipes out this thing. It amounts to clear reasoning! Here are two eyes. Were they meant to see nothing but one side! Here is a tongue with a line down the middle almost to the tip of it—which is for service. That Beppo couldn't deal double, if he would; for he is imperfectly designed—a mere dog's pattern! But, only one heart, signorina—mind that. I will never forget the cigarette. I shall smoke it before I leave the mountain, and think— oh!"

Having illustrated the philosophy of his system, Luigi continued: "I am going to tell you everything. Pray, do not look on Beppo! This is important. The Signor Antonio-Pericles sent me to spy on you, because he expects some people to come up the mountain, and you know them; and one is an Austrian officer, and he is an Englishman by birth, and he is coming to meet some English friends who enter Italy from Switzerland over the Moro, and easily up here on mules or donkeys from Pella. The Signor Antonio-Pericles has gold ears for everything that concerns the signorina. "A patriot is she!" he says; and he is jealous of your English friends. He thinks they will distract you from your studies; and perhaps"—Luigi nodded sagaciously before he permitted himself to say— "perhaps he is jealous in another way. I have heard him speak like a sonnet of the signorina's beauty. The Signor Antonio-Pericles thinks that you have come here to-day to meet them. When he heard that you were going to leave Milan for Baveno, he was mad, and with two fists up, against all English persons. The Englishman who is an Austrian officer is quartered at Verona, and the Signor Antonio-Pericles said that the Englishman should not meet you yet, if he could help it."

Victoria stood brooding. "Who can it be,—who is an
Englishman, and an
Austrian officer, and knows me?"

"Signorina, I don't know names. Behold, that Beppo is approaching like the snow! What I entreat is, that the signorina will wait a little for the English party, if they come, so that I may have something to tell my patron. To invent upon nothing is most unpleasant, and the Signor Antonio can soon perceive whether one swims with corks. Signorina, I can dance on one rope—I am a man. I am not a midge—I cannot dance upon nothing."

The days of Vittoria's youth had been passed in England. It was not unknown to her that old English friends were on the way to Italy; the recollection of a quiet and a buried time put a veil across her features. She was perplexed by the mention of the Austrian officer by Luigi, as one may be who divines the truth too surely, but will not accept it for its loathsomeness. There were Englishmen in the army of Austria. Could one of them be this one whom she had cared for when she was a girl? It seemed hatefully cruel to him to believe it. She spoke to Agostino, begging him to remain with her on the height awhile to see whether the Signor Antonio-Pericles was right; to see whether Luigi was a truth- teller; to see whether these English persons were really coming. "Because," she said, "if they do come, it will at once dissolve any suspicions you may have of this Luigi. And I always long so much to know if the Signor Antonio is correct. I have never yet known him to be wrong."

"And you want to see these English," said Agostino. He frowned.

"Only to hear them. They shall not recognize me. I have now another name; and I am changed. My hat is enough to hide me. Let me hear them talk a little. You and the Signor Carlo will stay with me, and when they come, if they do come, I will remain no longer than just sufficient to make sure. I would refuse to know any of them before the night of the fifteenth; I want my strength too much. I shall have to hear a misery from them; I know it, I feel it; it turns my blood. But let me hear their voices! England is half my country, though I am so willing to forget her and give all my life to Italy. Stay with me, dear friend, my best father! humour me, for you know that I am always charming when I am humoured."

Agostino pressed his finger on a dimple in her cheeks. "You can afford to make such a confession as that to a greybeard. The day is your own. Bear in mind that you are so situated that it will be prudent for you to have no fresh relations, either with foreigners or others, until your work is done,—in which, my dear child, may God bless you!"

"I pray to him with all my might," Vittoria said in reply.

After a consultation with Agostino, Ugo Corte and Marco and Giulio bade their adieux to her. The task of keeping Luigi from their clutches was difficult; but Agostino helped her in that also. To assure them, after his fashion, of the harmlessness of Luigi, he seconded him in a contest of wit against Beppo, and the little fellow, now that he had shaken off his fears, displayed a quickness of retort and a liveliness "unknown to professional spies and impossible to the race," said Agostino; "so absolutely is the mind of man blunted by Austrian gold. We know that for a fact. Beppo is no match for him. Beppo is sententious; ponderously illustrative; he can't turn; he is long-winded; he, I am afraid, my Carlo, studies the journals. He has got your journalistic style, wherein words of six syllables form the relief to words of eight, and hardly one dares to stand by itself. They are like huge boulders across a brook. The meaning, do you, see, would run of itself, but you give us these impedimenting big stones to help us over it, while we profess to understand you by implication. For my part, I own, that to me, your parliamentary, illegitimate academic, modern crocodile phraseology, which is formidable in the jaws, impenetrable on the back, can't circumvent a corner, and is enabled to enter a common understanding solely by having a special highway prepared for it,—in short, the writing in your journals is too much for me. Beppo here is an example that the style is useless for controversy. This Luigi baffles him at every step."

"Some," rejoined Carlo, "say that Beppo has had the virtue to make you his study."

Agostino threw himself on his back and closed his eyes. "That, then, is more than you have done, signor Tuquoque. Look on the Bernina yonder, and fancy you behold a rout of phantom Goths; a sleepy rout, new risen, with the blood of old battles on their shroud-shirts, and a North-east wind blowing them upon our fat land. Or take a turn at the other side toward Orta, and look out for another invasion, by no means so picturesque, but preferable. Tourists! Do you hear them?"

Carlo Ammiani had descried the advanced troop of a procession of gravely- heated climbers ladies upon donkeys, and pedestrian guards stalking beside them, with courier, and lacqueys, and baskets of provisions, all bearing the stamp of pilgrims from the great Western Island.

CHAPTER VI
THE WARNING

A mountain ascended by these children of the forcible Isle, is a mountain to be captured, and colonized, and absolutely occupied for a term; so that Vittoria soon found herself and her small body of adherents observed, and even exclaimed against, as a sort of intruding aborigines, whose presence entirely dispelled the sense of romantic dominion which a mighty eminence should give, and which Britons expect when they have expended a portion of their energies. The exclamations were not complimentary; nevertheless, Vittoria listened with pleased ears, as one listens by a brookside near an old home, hearing a music of memory rather than common words. They talked of heat, of appetite, of chill, of thirst, of the splendour of the prospect, of the anticipations of good hotel accommodation below, of the sadness superinduced by the reflection that in these days people were found everywhere, and poetry was thwarted; again of heat, again of thirst, of beauty, and of chill. There was the enunciation of matronly advice; there was the outcry of girlish insubordination; there were sighings for English ale, and namings of the visible ranges of peaks, and indicatings of geographical fingers to show where Switzerland and Piedmont met, and Austria held her grasp on Lombardy; and "to this point we go to-night; yonder to-morrow; farther the next day," was uttered, soberly or with excitement, as befitted the age of the speaker.

Among these tourists there was one very fair English lady, with long auburn curls of the traditionally English pattern, and the science of Paris displayed in her bonnet and dress; which, if not as graceful as severe admirers of the antique in statuary or of the mediaeval in drapery demand, pleads prettily to be thought so, and commonly succeeds in its object, when assisted by an artistic feminine manner. Vittoria heard her answer to the name of Mrs. Sedley. She had once known her as a Miss Adela Pole. Amidst the cluster of assiduous gentlemen surrounding this lady it was difficult for Vittoria's stolen glances to discern her husband; and the moment she did discern him she became as indifferent to him as was his young wife, by every manifestation of her sentiments. Mrs. Sedley informed her lord that it was not expected of him to care, or to pretend to care, for such scenes as the Motterone exhibited; and having dismissed him to the shade of an umbrella near the provision baskets, she took her station within a few steps of Vittoria, and allowed her attendant gentlemen to talk while she remained plunged in a meditative rapture at the prospect. The talk indicated a settled scheme for certain members of the party to reach Milan from the Como road. Mrs. Sedley was asked if she expected her brother to join her here or in Milan.

"Here, if a man's promises mean anything," she replied languidly.

She was told that some one waved a handkerchief to them from below.

"Is he alone?" she said; and directing an operaglass upon the slope of the mountain, pursued, as in a dreamy disregard of circumstances: "That is Captain Gambier. My brother Wilfrid has not kept his appointment. Perhaps he could not get leave from the General; perhaps he is married; he is engaged to an Austrian Countess, I have heard. Captain Gambier did me the favour to go round to a place called Stresa to meet him. He has undertaken the journey for nothing. It is the way with all journeys though this" (the lady had softly reverted to her rapture) "this is too exquisite! Nature at least does not deceive."

Vittoria listened to a bubbling of meaningless chatter, until Captain Gambier had joined Mrs. Sedley; and at him, for she had known him likewise, she could not forbear looking up. He was speaking to Mrs. Sedley, but caught the look, and bent his head for a clearer view of the features under the broad straw hat. Mrs. Sedley commanded him imperiously to say on.

"Have you no letter from Wilfrid? Has the mountain tired you? Has Wilfrid failed to send his sister one word? Surely Mr. Pericles will have made known our exact route to him? And his uncle, General Pierson, could—I am certain he did—exert his influence to procure him leave for a single week to meet the dearest member of his family."

Captain Gambier gathered his wits to give serviceable response to the kindled lady, and letting his eyes fall from time to time on the broad straw hat, made answer—

"Lieutenant Pierson, or, in other words, Wilfrid Pole—"

The lady stamped her foot and flushed.

"You know, Augustus, I detest that name."

"Pardon me a thousandfold. I had forgotten."

"What has happened to you?"

Captain Gambier accused the heat.

"I found a letter from Wilfrid at the hotel. He is apparently kept on constant service between Milan, and Verona, and Venice. His quarters are at Verona. He informs me that he is to be married in the Spring; that is, if all continues quiet; married in the Spring. He seems to fancy that there may be disturbances; not of a serious kind, of course. He will meet you in Milan. He has never been permitted to remain at Milan longer than a couple of days at a stretch. Pericles has told him that she is in Florence. Pericles has told me that Miss Belloni has removed to Florence."

"Say it a third time," the lady indulgently remarked.

"I do not believe that she has gone."

"I dare say not."

"She has changed her name, you know."

"Oh, dear, yes; she has done something fantastic, naturally! For my part, I should have thought her own good enough."

"Emilia Alessandra Belloni is good enough, certainly," said Captain Gambier.

The shading straw rim had shaken once during the colloquy. It was now a fixed defence.

"What is her new name?" Mrs. Sedley inquired.

"That I cannot tell. Wilfrid merely mentions that he has not seen her."

"I," said Mrs. Sedley, "when I reach Milan, shall not trust to Mr. Pericles, but shall write to the Conservatorio; for if she is going to be a great cantatrice, really, it will be agreeable to renew acquaintance with her. Nor will it do any mischief to Wilfrid, now that he is engaged. Are you very deeply attached to straw hats? They are sweet in a landscape."

Mrs. Sedley threw him a challenge from her blue eyes; but his reply to it was that of an unskilled youth, who reads a lady by the letters of her speech:—"One minute. I will be with you instantly. I want to have a look down on the lake. I suppose this is one of the most splendid views in Italy. Half a minute!"

Captain Gambier smiled brilliantly; and the lady, perceiving that polished shield, checked the shot of indignation on her astonished features, and laid it by. But the astonishment lingered there, like the lines of a slackened bow. She beheld her ideal of an English gentleman place himself before these recumbent foreign people, and turn to talk across them, with a pertinacious pursuit of the face under the bent straw hat. Nor was it singular to her that one of them at last should rise and protest against the continuation of the impertinence.

Carlo Ammiani, in fact, had opened matters with a scrupulously-courteous bow.

"Monsieur is perhaps unaware that he obscures the outlook?"

"Totally, monsieur," said Captain Gambier, and stood fast.

"Will monsieur do me the favour to take three steps either to the right or to the left?"

"Pardon, monsieur, but the request is put almost in the form of an order."

"Simply if it should prove inefficacious in the form of a request."

"What, may I ask, monsieur, is your immediate object?"

"To entreat you to behave with civility."

"I am at a loss, monsieur, to perceive any offence."

"Permit me to say, it is lamentable you do not know when you insult a lady."

"I have insulted a lady?" Captain Gambier looked profoundly incredulous. "Oh! then you will not take exception to my assuming the privilege to apologize to her in person?"

Ammiani arrested him as he was about to pass.

"Stay, monsieur; you determine to be impudent, I perceive; you shall not be obtrusive."

Vittoria had tremblingly taken old Agostino's hand, and had risen to her feet. Still keeping her face hidden, she walked down the slope, followed at an interval by her servant, and curiously watched by the English officer, who said to himself, "Well, I suppose I was mistaken," and consequently discovered that he was in a hobble.

A short duologue in their best stilted French ensued between him and Ammiani. It was pitched too high in a foreign tongue for Captain Gambier to descend from it, as he would fain have done, to ask the lady's name. They exchanged cards and formal salutes, and parted.

The dignified altercation had been witnessed by the main body of the tourists. Captain Gambier told them that he had merely interchanged amicable commonplaces with the Frenchman,—"or Italian," he added carelessly, reading the card in his hand. "I thought she might be somebody whom we knew," he said to Mrs. Sedley.

"Not the shadow of a likeness to her," the lady returned.

She had another opinion when later a scrap of paper bearing one pencilled line on it was handed round. A damsel of the party had picked it up near the spot where, as she remarked, "the foreigners had been sitting." It said:—

"Let none who look for safety go to Milan."

CHAPTER VII
BARTO RIZZO

A week following the day of meetings on the Motterone, Luigi the spy was in Milan, making his way across the Piazza de' Mercanti. He entered a narrow court, one of those which were anciently built upon the Oriental principle of giving shade at the small cost of excluding common air. It was dusky noon there through the hours of light, and thrice night when darkness fell. The atmosphere, during the sun's short passage overhead, hung with a glittering heaviness, like the twinkling iron-dust in a subterranean smithy. On the lower window of one of the houses there was a board, telling men that Barto Rizzo made and mended shoes, and requesting people who wished to see him to make much noise at the door, for he was hard of hearing. It speedily became known in the court that a visitor desired to see Barto Rizzo. The noise produced by Luigi was like that of a fanatical beater of the tomtom; he knocked and banged and danced against the door, crying out for his passing amusement an adaptation of a popular ballad:—

"Oh, Barto, Barto! my boot is sadly worn: The toe is seen that should be veiled from sight. The toe that should be veiled like an Eastern maid: like a sultan's daughter: Shocking! shocking! One of a company of ten that were living a secluded life in chaste privacy! Oh, Barto, Barto! must I charge it to thy despicable leather or to my incessant pilgrimages? One fair toe! I fear presently the corruption of the remaining nine: Then, alas! what do I go on? How shall I come to a perfumed end, who walk on ten indecent toes? Well may the delicate gentlemen sneer at me and scorn me: As for the angelic Lady who deigns to look so low, I may say of her that her graciousness clothes what she looks at: To her the foot, the leg, the back: To her the very soul is bared: But she is a rarity upon earth. Oh, Barto, Barto, she is rarest in

Milan! I might run a day's length and not find her. If, O Barto, as my boot hints to me, I am about to be stripped of my last covering, I must hurry to the inconvenient little chamber of my mother, who cannot refuse to acknowledge me as of this pattern: Barto, O shoemaker! thou son of artifice and right-hand-man of necessity, preserve me in the fashion of the time: Cobble me neatly: A dozen wax threads and I am remade:—Excellent! I thank you! Now I can plant my foot bravely: Oh, Barto, my shoemaker! between ourselves, it is unpleasant in these refined days to be likened at all to that preposterous Adam!"

The omission of the apostrophes to Barto left it one of the ironical, veiled Republican, semi-socialistic ballads of the time, which were sung about the streets for the sharpness and pith of the couplets, and not from a perception of the double edge down the length of them.

As Luigi was coming to the terminating line, the door opened. A very handsome sullen young woman, of the dark, thick-browed Lombard type, asked what was wanted; at the same time the deep voice of a man; conjecturally rising from a lower floor, called, and a lock was rattled. The woman told Luigi to enter. He sent a glance behind him; he had evidently been drained of his sprightliness in a second; he moved in with the slackness of limb of a gibbeted figure. The door shut; the woman led him downstairs. He could not have danced or sung a song now for great pay. The smell of mouldiness became so depressing to him that the smell of leather struck his nostrils refreshingly. He thought: "Oh, Virgin! it's dark enough to make one believe in every single thing they tell us about the saints." Up in the light of day Luigi had a turn for careless thinking on these holy subjects.

Barto Rizzo stood before him in a square of cellarage that was furnished with implements of his craft, too dark for a clear discernment of features.

"So, here you are!" was the greeting Luigi received.

It was a tremendous voice, that seemed to issue from a vast cavity. "Lead the gentleman to my sitting-room," said Barto. Luigi felt the wind of a handkerchief, and guessed that his eyes were about to be bandaged by the woman behind him. He petitioned to be spared it, on the plea, firstly, that it expressed want of confidence; secondly, that it took him in the stomach. The handkerchief was tight across his eyes while he was speaking. His hand was touched by the woman, and he commenced timidly an ascent of stairs. It continued so that he would have sworn he was a shorter time going up the Motterone; then down, and along a passage; lower down, deep into corpse-climate; up again, up another enormous mountain; and once more down, as among rats and beetles, and down, as among faceless horrors, and down, where all things seemed prostrate and with a taste of brass. It was the poor fellow's nervous imagination, preternaturally excited. When the handkerchief was caught away, his jaw was shuddering, his eyes were sickly; he looked as if impaled on the prongs of fright. It required just half a minute to reanimate this mercurial creature, when he found himself under the light of two lamps, and Barto Rizzo fronting him, in a place so like the square of cellarage which he had been led to with unbandaged eyes, that it relieved his dread by touching his humour. He cried, "Have I made the journey of the Signor Capofinale, who visited the other end of the world by standing on his head?"

Barto Rizzo rolled out a burly laugh.

"Sit," he said. "You're a poor sweating body, and must needs have a dry tongue. Will you drink?"

"Dry!" quoth Luigi. "Holy San Carlo is a mash in a wine-press compared with me."

Barto Rizzo handed him a liquor, which he drank, and after gave thanks to Providence. Barto raised his hand.

"We're too low down here for that kind of machinery," he said. "They say that Providence is on the side of the Austrians. Now then, what have you to communicate to me? This time I let you come to my house trust at all, trust entirely. I think that's the proverb. You are admitted: speak like a guest."

Luigi's preference happened to be for categorical interrogations. Never having an idea of spontaneously telling the whole truth, the sense that he was undertaking a narrative gave him such emotions as a bad swimmer upon deep seas may have; while, on the other hand, his being subjected to a series of questions seemed at least to leave him with one leg on shore, for then he could lie discreetly, and according to the finger-posts, and only when necessary, and he could recover himself if he made a false step. His ingenious mind reasoned these images out to his own satisfaction. He requested, therefore, that his host would let him hear what he desired to know.

Barto Rizzo's forefinger was pressed from an angle into one temple. His head inclined to meet it: so that it was like the support to a broad blunt pillar. The cropped head was flat as an owl's; the chest of immense breadth; the bulgy knees and big hands were those of a dwarf athlete. Strong colour, lying full on him from the neck to the forehead, made the big veins purple and the eyes fierier than the movements of his mind would have indicated. He was simply studying the character of his man. Luigi feared him; he was troubled chiefly because he was unaware of what Barto Rizzo wanted to know, and could not consequently tell what to bring to the market. The simplicity of the questions put to him was bewildering: he fell into the trap. Barto's eyes began to get terribly oblique. Jingling money in his pocket, he said:—

"You saw Colonel Corte on the Motterone: you saw the Signor Agostino Balderini: good men, both! Also young Count Ammiani: I served his father, the General, and jogged the lad on my knee. You saw the Signorina Vittoria. The English people came, and you heard them talk, but did not understand. You came home and told all this to the Signor Antonio, your employer number one. You have told the same to me, your employer number two. There's your pay."

Barto summed up thus the information he had received, and handed Luigi six gold pieces. The latter, springing with boyish thankfulness and pride at the easy earning of them, threw in a few additional facts, as, that he had been taken for a spy by the conspirators, and had heard one of the Englishmen mention the Signorina Vittoria's English name. Barto Rizzo lifted his eyebrows queerly. "We'll go through another interrogatory in an hour," he said; "stop here till I return."

Luigi was always too full of his own cunning to suspect the same in another, until he was left alone to reflect on a scene; when it became overwhelmingly transparent. "But, what could I say more than I did say?" he asked himself, as he stared at the one lamp Barto had left. Finding the door unfastened, he took the lamp and lighted himself out, and along a cavernous passage ending in a blank wall, against which his heart knocked and fell, for his sensation was immediately the terror of imprisonment and helplessness. Mad with alarm, he tried every spot for an aperture. Then he sat down on his haunches; he remembered hearing word of Barto Rizzo's rack: — certain methods peculiar to Barto Rizzo, by which he screwed matters out of his agents, and terrified them into fidelity. His personal dealings with Barto were of recent date; but Luigi knew him by repute: he knew that the shoemaking business was a mask. Barto had been a soldier, a schoolmaster: twice an exile; a conspirator since the day when the Austrians had the two fine Apples of Pomona, Lombardy and Venice, given them as fruits of peace. Luigi remembered how he had snapped his fingers at the name of Barto Rizzo. There was no despising him now. He could only arrive at a peaceful contemplation of Barto Rizzo's character by determining to tell all, and (since that seemed little) more than he knew. He got back to the leather-smelling chamber, which was either the same or purposely rendered exactly similar to the one he had first been led to.

At the end of a leaden hour Barto Rizzo returned.

"Now, to recommence," he said. "Drink before you speak, if your tongue is dry."

Luigi thrust aside the mention of liquor. It seemed to him that by doing so he propitiated that ill-conceived divinity called Virtue, who lived in the open air, and desired men to drink water. Barto Rizzo evidently understood the kind of man he was schooling to his service.

"Did that Austrian officer, who is an Englishman, acquainted with the Signor Antonio-Pericles, meet the lady, his sister, on the Motterone?"

Luigi answered promptly, "Yes."

"Did the Signorina Vittoria speak to the lady?"

"No."

"Not a word?"

"No."

"Not one communication to her?"

"No: she sat under her straw hat."

"She concealed her face?"

"She sat like a naughty angry girl."

"Did she speak to the officer?"

"Not she!"

"Did she see him?"

"Of course she did! As if a woman's eyes couldn't see through straw- plait!"

Barto paused, calculatingly, eye on victim.

"The Signorina Vittoria," he resumed, "has engaged to sing on the night of the Fifteenth; has she?"

A twitching of Luigi's muscles showed that he apprehended a necessary straining of his invention on another tack.

"On the night of the Fifteenth, Signor Barto Rizzo? That's the night of her first appearance. Oh, yes!"

"To sing a particular song?"

"Lots of them! ay-ay!"

Barto took him by the shoulder and pressed him into his seat till he howled, saying, "Now, there's a slate and a pencil. Expect me at the end of two hours, this time. Next time it will be four: then eight, then sixteen. Find out how many hours that will be at the sixteenth examination."

Luigi flew at the torturer and stuck at the length of his straightened arm, where he wriggled, refusing to listen to the explanation of Barto's system; which was that, in cases where every fresh examination taught him more, they were continued, after regularly-lengthening intervals, that might extend from the sowing of seed to the ripening of grain. "When all's delivered," said Barto, "then we begin to correct discrepancies. I expect," he added, "you and I will have done before a week's out."

"A week!" Luigi shouted. "Here's my stomach already leaping like a fish at the smell of this hole. You brute bear! it's a smell of bones. It turns my inside with a spoon. May the devil seize you when you're sleeping! You shan't go: I'll tell you everything—everything. I can't tell you anything more than I have told you. She gave me a cigarette—there! Now you know:—gave me a cigarette; a cigarette. I smoked it— there! Your faithful servant!"

"She gave you a cigarette, and you smoked it; ha!" said Barto Rizzo, who appeared to see something to weigh even in that small fact. "The English lady gave you the cigarette?"

Luigi nodded: "Yes;" pertinacious in deception. "Yes," he repeated; "the English lady. That was the person. What's the use of your skewering me with your eyes!"

"I perceive that you have never travelled, my Luigi," said Barto. "I am afraid we shall not part so early as I had supposed. I double the dose, and return to you in four hours' time."

Luigi threw himself flat on the ground, shrieking that he was ready to tell everything—anything. Not even the apparent desperation of his circumstances could teach him that a promise to tell the truth was a more direct way of speaking. Indeed, the hitting of the truth would have seemed to him a sort of artful archery, the burden of which should devolve upon the questioner, whom he supplied with the relation of "everything and anything."

All through a night Luigi's lesson continued. In the morning he was still breaking out in small and purposeless lies; but Barto Rizzo had accomplished his two objects: that of squeezing him, and that of subjecting his imagination. Luigi confessed (owing to a singular recovery of his memory) the gift of the cigarette as coming from the Signorina Vittoria. What did it matter if she did give him a cigarette?

"You adore her for it?" said Barto.

"May the Virgin sweep the floor of heaven into her lap!" interjected Luigi. "She is a good patriot."

"Are you one?" Barto asked.

"Certainly I am."

"Then I shall have to suspect you, for the good of your country."

Luigi could not see the deduction. He was incapable of guessing that it might apply forcibly to Vittoria, who had undertaken a grave, perilous, and imminent work. Nothing but the spontaneous desire to elude the pursuit of a questioner had at first instigated his baffling of Barto Rizzo, until, fearing the dark square man himself, he feared him dimly for Vittoria's sake; he could not have said why. She was a good patriot: wherefore the reason for wishing to know more of her? Barto Rizzo had compelled him at last to furnish a narrative of the events of that day on the Motterone, and, finding himself at sea, Luigi struck out boldly and swam as well as he could. Barto disentangled one succinct thread of incidents: Vittoria had been commissioned by the Chief to sing on the night of the Fifteenth; she had subsequently, without speaking to any of the English party, or revealing her features "keeping them beautifully hidden," Luigi said, with unaccountable enthusiasm – written a warning to them that they were to avoid Milan. The paper on which the warning had been written was found by the English when he was the only Italian on the height, lying thereto observe and note things in the service of Barto Rizzo. The writing was English, but when one of the English ladies – "who wore her hair like a planed shred of wood; like a torn vine; like a kite with two tails; like Luxury at the Banquet, ready to tumble over marble shoulders" (an illustration drawn probably from Luigi's study of some allegorical picture, – he was at a loss to describe the foreign female head-dress) – when this lady had read the writing, she exclaimed that it was the hand of "her Emilia!" and soon after she addressed Luigi in English, then in French, then in "barricade Italian" (by which phrase Luigi meant that the Italian words were there, but did not present their proper smooth footing for his understanding), and strove to obtain information from him concerning the signorina, and also concerning the chances that Milan would be an agitated city. Luigi assured her that Milan was the peacefullest of cities – a pure babe. He admitted his acquaintance with the Signorina Vittoria Campa, and denied her being "any longer" the Emilia Alessandra Belloni of the English lady. The latter had partly retained him in her service, having given him directions to call at her hotel in Milan, and help her to communicate with her old friend. "I present myself to her to-morrow, Friday," said Luigi.

"That's to-day," said Barto.

Luigi clapped his hand to his cheek, crying wofully, "You've drawn, beastly gaoler! a night out of my life like an old jaw-tooth."

"There's day two or three fathoms above us," said Barto; "and hot coffee is coming down."

"I believe I've been stewing in a pot while the moon looked so cool." Luigi groaned, and touched up along the sleeves of his arms: that which he fancied he instantaneously felt.

The coffee was brought by the heavy-browed young woman. Before she quitted the place Barto desired her to cast her eyes on Luigi, and say whether she thought she should know him again. She scarcely glanced, and gave answer with a shrug of the shoulders as she retired. Luigi at the time was drinking. He rose; he was about to speak, but yawned instead. The woman's carelessly-dropped upper eyelids seemed to him to be reading him through a dozen of his contortions and disguises, and checked the idea of liberty which he associated with getting to the daylight.

"But it is worth the money!" shouted Barto Rizzo, with a splendid divination of his thought. "You skulker! are you not paid and fattened to do business which you've only to remember, and it'll honey your legs in purgatory? You're the shooting-dog of that Greek, and you nose about the bushes for his birds, and who cares if any fellow, just for exercise, shoots a dagger a yard from his wrist and sticks you in the back? You serve me, and there's pay for you; brothers, doctors, nurses, friends,—a tight blanket if you fall from a housetop! and masses for your soul when your hour strikes. The treacherous cur lies rotting in a ditch! Do you conceive that when I employ you I am in your power? Your intelligence will open gradually. Do you know that here in this house I can conceal fifty men, and leave the door open to the Croats to find them? I tell you now—you are free; go forth. You go alone; no one touches you; ten years hence a skeleton is found with an English letter on its ribs—"

"Oh, stop! signor Barto, and be a blessed man," interposed Luigi, doubling and wriggling in a posture that appeared as if he were shaking negatives from the elbows of his crossed arms. "Stop. How did you know of a letter? I forgot—I have seen the English lady at her hotel. I was carrying the signorina's answer, when I thought "Barto Rizzo calls me," and I came like a lamb. And what does it matter? She is a good patriot; you are a good patriot; here it is. Consider my reputation, do; and be careful with the wax."

Barto drew a long breath. The mention of the English letter had been a shot in the dark. The result corroborated his devotional belief in the unerringness of his own powerful intuition. He had guessed the case, or hardly even guessed it—merely stated it, to horrify Luigi. The letter was placed in his hands, and he sat as strongly thrilled by emotion, under the mask of his hard face, as a lover hearing music. "I read English," he remarked.

After he had drawn the seal three or four times slowly over the lamp, the green wax bubbled and unsnapped. Vittoria had written the following lines in reply to her old English friend:—

"Forgive me, and do not ask to see me until we have passed the fifteenth of the month. You will see me that night at La Scala. I wish to embrace you, but I am miserable to think of your being in Milan. I cannot yet tell you where my residence is. I have not met your brother. If he writes to me it will make me happy, but I refuse to see him. I will explain to him why. Let him not try to see me. Let him send by this messenger. I hope he will contrive to be out of Milan all this month. Pray let me influence you to go for a time. I write coldly; I am tired, and forget my English. I do not forget my friends. I have you close against my heart. If it were prudent, and it involved me alone, I would come to you without a moment's loss of time. Do know that I am not changed, and am your affectionate

"Emilia."

When Barto Rizzo had finished reading, he went from the chamber and blew his voice into what Luigi supposed to be a hollow tube.

"This letter," he said, coming back, "is a repetition of the Signorina Vittoria's warning to her friends on the Motterone. The English lady's brother, who is in the Austrian service, was there, you say?"

Luigi considered that, having lately been believed in, he could not afford to look untruthful, and replied with a sprightly "Assuredly."

"He was there, and he read the writing on the paper?"

"Assuredly: right out loud, between puff-puff of his cigar."

"His name is Lieutenant Pierson. Did not Antonio-Pericles tell you his name? He will write to her: you will be the bearer of his letter to the signorina. I must see her reply. She is a good patriot; so am I; so are you. Good patriots must be prudent. I tell you, I must see her reply to this Lieutenant Pierson." Barto stuck his thumb and finger astride Luigi's shoulder and began rocking him gently, with a horrible meditative expression. "You will have to accomplish this, my Luigi. All fair excuses will be made, if you fail generally. This you must do. Keep upright while I am speaking to you! The excuses will be made; but I, not you, must make them: bear that in mind. Is there any person whom you, my Luigi, like best in the world?"

It was a winning question, and though Luigi was not the dupe of its insinuating gentleness, he answered, "The little girl who carries flowers every morning to the caffe La Scala."

"Ah! the little girl who carries flowers every morning to the caffe La Scala. Now, my Luigi, you may fail me, and I may pardon you. Listen attentively: if you are false; if you are guilty of one piece of treachery:—do you see? You can't help slipping, but you can help jumping. Restrain yourself from jumping, that's all. If you are guilty of treachery, hurry at once, straight off, to the little girl who carries flowers every morning to the caffe La Scala. Go to her, take her by the two cheeks, kiss her, say to her 'addio, addio,' for, by the thunder of heaven! you will never see her more."

Luigi was rocked forward and back, while Barto spoke in level tones, till the voice dropped into its vast hollow, when Barto held him fast a moment, and hurled him away by the simple lifting of his hand.

The woman appeared and bound Luigi's eyes. Barto did not utter another word. On his journey back to daylight, Luigi comforted himself by muttering oaths that he would never again enter into this trap. As soon as his eyes were unbandaged, he laughed, and sang, and tossed a compliment from his finger-tips to the savage-browed beauty; pretended that he had got an armful, and that his heart was touched by the ecstasy; and sang again: "Oh, Barto, Barto! my boot is sadly worn. The toe is seen," etc., half-way down the stanzas. Without his knowing it, and before he had quitted the court, he had sunk into songless gloom, brooding on the scenes of the night. However free he might be in body, his imagination was captive to Barto Rizzo. He was no luckier than a bird, for whom the cage is open that it may feel the more keenly with its little taste of liberty that it is tied by the leg.

CHAPTER VIII
THE LETTER

The importance of the matters extracted from Luigi does not lie on the surface; it will have to be seen through Barto Rizzo's mind. This man regarded himself as the mainspring of the conspiracy; specially its guardian, its wakeful Argus. He had conspired sleeplessly for thirty years; so long, that having no ideal reserve in his nature, conspiracy had become his professional occupation,—the wheel which it was his business to roll. He was above jealousy; he was above vanity. No one outstripping him cast a bad colour on him; nor did he object to bow to another as his superior. But he was prepared to suspect every one of insincerity and of faithlessness; and, being the master of the machinery of the plots, he was ready, upon a whispered justification, to despise the orders of his leader, and act by his own light in blunt disobedience. For it was his belief that while others speculated he knew all. He knew where the plots had failed; he knew the man who had bent and doubled. In the patriotic cause, perfect arrangements are crowned with perfect success, unless there is an imperfection of the instruments; for the cause is blessed by all superior agencies. Such was his governing idea. His arrangements had always been perfect; hence the deduction was a denunciation of some one particular person. He pointed out the traitor here, the traitor there; and in one or two cases he did so with a mildness that made those fret at their beards vaguely who understood his character. Barto Rizzo was, it was said, born in a village near Forli, in the dominions of the Pope; according to the rumour, he was the child of a veiled woman and a cowled paternity. If not an offender against Government, he was at least a wanderer early in life. None could accuse him of personal ambition. He boasted that he had served as a common soldier with the Italian contingent furnished by Eugene to the Moscow campaign; he showed scars of old wounds: brown spots, and blue spots, and twisted twine of white skin, dotting the wrist, the neck, the calf, the ankle, and looking up from them, he slapped them proudly. Nor had he personal animosities of any kind. One sharp scar, which he called his shoulder knot, he owed to the knife of a friend, by name Sarpo, who had things ready to betray him, and struck him, in anticipation of that tremendous moment of surprise and wrath when the awakened victim frequently is nerved with devil's strength; but, striking, like a novice, on the bone, the stilet stuck there; and Barto coolly got him to point the outlet of escape, and walked off, carrying the blade where the terrified assassin had planted it. This Sarpo had become a tradesman in Milan—a bookseller and small printer; and he was unmolested. Barto said of him, that he was as bad as a few odd persons thought himself to be, and had in him the making of a great traitor; but, that as Sarpo hated him and had sought to be rid of him for private reasons only, it was a pity to waste on such a fellow steel that should serve the Cause. "While I live," said Barto, "my enemies have a tolerably active conscience."

The absence of personal animosity in him was not due to magnanimity. He doubted the patriotism of all booksellers. He had been twice betrayed by women. He never attempted to be revenged on them; but he doubted the patriotism of all women. "Use them; keep eye on them," he said. In Venice he had conspired when he was living there as the clerk of a notary; in Bologna subsequently while earning his bread as a petty schoolmaster. His evasions, both of Papal sbirri and the Austrian polizia, furnished instances of astonishing audacity that made his name a byword for mastery in the hour of peril. His residence in Milan now, after seven years of exile in England and Switzerland, was an act of pointed defiance, incomprehensible to his own party, and only to be explained by the prevalent belief that the authorities feared to provoke a collision with the people by laying hands on him. They had only once made a visitation to his house, and appeared to be satisfied at not finding him. At that period Austria was simulating benevolence in her Lombardic provinces, with the half degree of persuasive earnestness which makes a Government lax in its vigilance, and leaves it simply open to the charge of effeteness. There were contradictory rumours as to whether his house had ever been visited by the polizia; but it was a legible fact that his name was on the window, and it was understood that he was not without elusive contrivances in the event of the authorities declaring war against him.

Of the nature of these contrivances Luigi had just learnt something. He had heard Barto Rizzo called 'The Miner' and 'The Great Cat,' and he now comprehended a little of the quality of his employer. He had entered a very different service from that of the Signor Antonio-Pericles, who paid him for nothing more than to keep eye on Vittoria, and recount her goings in and out; for what absolute object he was unaware, but that it was not for a political one he was certain. "Cursed be the day when the lust of gold made me open my hand to Barto Rizzo!" he thought; and could only reflect that life is short and gold is sweet, and that he was in the claws of the Great Cat. He had met Barto in a wine-shop. He cursed the habit which led him to call at that shop; the thirst which tempted him to drink: the ear which had been seduced to listen. Yet as all his expenses had been paid in advance, and his reward at the instant of his application for it; and as the signorina and Barto were both good patriots, and he, Luigi, was a good patriot, what harm could be done to her? Both she and Barto had stamped their different impressions on his waxen nature. He reconciled his service to them separately by the exclamation that they were both good patriots.

The plot for the rising in Milan city was two months old. It comprised some of the nobles of the city, and enjoyed the good wishes of the greater part of them, whose payment of fifty to sixty per cent to the Government on the revenue of their estates was sufficient reason for a desire to change masters, positively though they might detest Republicanism, and dread the shadow of anarchy. These looked hopefully to Charles Albert. Their motive was to rise, or to countenance a rising, and summon the ambitious Sardinian monarch with such assurances of devotion, that a Piedmontese army would be at the gates when the banner of Austria was in the dust. Among the most active members of the prospectively insurgent aristocracy of Milan was Count Medole, a young nobleman of vast wealth and possessed of a reliance on his powers of mind that induced him to take a prominent part in the opening deliberations, and speedily necessitated his hire of the friendly offices of one who could supply him with facts, with suggestions, with counsel, with fortitude, with everything to strengthen his pretensions to the leadership, excepting money. He discovered his man in Barto Rizzo, who quitted the ranks of the republican section to serve him, and wield a tool for his own party. By the help of Agostino Balderini, Carlo Ammiani, and others, the aristocratic and the republican sections of the conspiracy were brought near enough together to permit of a common action between them, though the maintaining of such harmony demanded an extreme and tireless delicacy of management. The presence of the Chief, whom we have seen on the Motterone, was claimed by other cities of Italy. Unto him solely did Barto Rizzo yield thorough adhesion. He being absent from Milan, Barto undertook to represent him and carry out his views. How far he was entitled to do so may be guessed when it is stated that, on the ground of his general contempt for women, he objected to the proposition that Vittoria should give the signal. The proposition was Agostino's. Count Medole, Barto, and Agostino discussed it secretly: Barto held resolutely against it, until Agostino thrust a sly-handed letter into his fingers and let him know that previous to any consultation on the subject he had gained the consent of his Chief. Barto then fell silent. He despatched his new spy, Luigi, to the Motterone, more for the purpose of giving him a schooling on the expedition, and on his return from it, and so getting hand and brain and soul service out of him. He expected no such a report of Vittoria's indiscretion as Luigi had spiced with his one foolish lie. That she should tell the relatives of an Austrian officer that Milan was soon to be a dangerous place for them;—and that she should write it on paper and leave it for the officer to read,—left her, according to Barto's reading of her, open to the alternative charges of imbecility or of treachery. Her letter to the English lady, the Austrian officer's sister, was an exaggeration of the offence, but lent it more the look of heedless folly. The point was to obtain sight of her letter to the Austrian officer himself. Barto was baffled during a course of anxious days that led closely up to the fifteenth. She had written no letter. Lieutenant Pierson, the officer in question, had ridden into the city once from Verona, and had called upon Antonio-Pericles to extract her address from him; the Greek had denied that she was in Milan. Luigi could tell no more. He described the officer's personal appearance, by saying that he was a recognizable Englishman in Austrian dragoon uniform;—white tunic, white helmet, brown moustache;—ay! and eh! and oh! and ah! coming frequently from his mouth; that he stood square while speaking, and seemed to like his own smile; an extraordinary touch of portraiture, or else a scoff at insular self-satisfaction; at any rate, it commended itself to the memory. Barto dismissed him, telling him to be daily in attendance on the English lady.

Barto Rizzo's respect for the Chief was at war with his intense conviction that a blow should be struck at Vittoria even upon the narrow information which he possessed. Twice betrayed, his dreams and haunting thoughts cried "Shall a woman betray you thrice?" In his imagination he stood identified with Italy: the betrayal of one meant that of both. Falling into a deep reflection, Barto counted over his hours of conspiracy: he counted the Chief's; comparing the two sets of figures he discovered, that as he had suspected, he was the elder in the patriotic work therefore, if he bowed his head to the Chief, it was a voluntary act, a form of respect, and not the surrendering of his judgement. He was on the spot: the Chief was absent. Barto reasoned that the Chief could have had no experience of women, seeing that he was ready to trust in them. "Do I trust to my pigeon, my sling-stone?" he said jovially to the thickbrowed, splendidly ruddy young woman, who was his wife; "do I trust her? Not half a morsel of her!" This young woman, a peasant woman of remarkable personal attractions, served him with the fidelity of a fascinated animal, and the dumbness of a wooden vessel. She could have hanged him, had it pleased her. She had all his secrets: but it was not vain speaking on Barto Rizzo's part; he was master of her will; and on the occasions when he showed that he did not trust her, he was careful at the same time to shock and subdue her senses. Her report of Vittoria was, that she went to the house of the Signora, Laura Piaveni, widow of the latest heroic son of Milan, and to that of the maestro Rocco Ricci; to no other. It was also Luigi's report.

"She's true enough," the woman said, evidently permitting herself to entertain an opinion; a sign that she required fresh schooling.

"So are you," said Barto, and eyed her in a way that made her ask, "Now, what's for me to do?"

He thought awhile.

"You will see the colonel. Tell him to come in corporal's uniform. What's the little wretch twisting her body for? Shan't I embrace her presently if she's obedient? Send to the polizia. You believe your husband is in the city, and will visit you in disguise at the corporal's hour. They seize him. They also examine the house up to the point where we seal it. Your object is to learn whether the Austrians are moving men upon Milan. If they are-I learn something. When the house has been examined, our court here will have rest for a good month ahead; and it suits me not to be disturbed. Do this, and we will have a red-wine evening in the house, shut up alone, my snake! my pepper-flower!"

It happened that Luigi was entering the court to keep an appointment with Barto when he saw a handful of the polizia burst into the house and drag out a soldier, who was in the uniform, as he guessed it to be, of the Prohaska regiment. The soldier struggled and offered money to them. Luigi could not help shouting, "You fools! don't you see he's an officer?" Two of them took their captive aside. The rest made a search through the house. While they were doing so Luigi saw Barto Rizzo's face at the windows of the house opposite. He clamoured at the door, but Barto was denied to him there. When the polizia had gone from the court, he was admitted and allowed to look into every room. Not finding him, he said, "Barto Rizzo does not keep his appointments, then!" The same words were repeated in his ear when he had left the court, and was in the street running parallel with it. "Barto Rizzo does not keep his appointments, then!" It was Barto who smacked him on the back, and spoke out his own name with brown-faced laughter in the bustling street. Luigi was so impressed by his cunning and his recklessness that he at once told him more than he wished to tell:—The Austrian officer was with his sister, and had written to the signorina, and Luigi had delivered the letter; but the signorina was at the maestro's, Rocco Ricci's, and there was no answer: the officer was leaving for Verona in the morning. After telling so much, Luigi drew back, feeling that he had given Barto his full measure and owed to the signorina what remained.

Barto probably read nothing of the mind of his spy, but understood that it was a moment for distrust of him. Vittoria and her mother lodged at the house of one Zotti, a confectioner, dwelling between the Duomo and La Scala. Luigi, at Barto's bidding, left word with Zotti that he would call for the signorina's answer to a certain letter about sunrise. "I promised my Rosellina, my poppyheaded sipper, a red-wine evening, or I would hold this fellow under my eye till the light comes," thought Barto misgivingly, and let him go. Luigi slouched about the English lady's hotel. At nightfall her brother came forth. Luigi directed him to be in the square of the Duomo by sunrise, and slipped from his hold; the officer ran after him some distance. "She can't say I was false to her now," said Luigi, dancing with nervous ecstasy. At sunrise Barto Rizzo was standing under the shadow of the Duomo. Luigi passed him and went to Zotti's house, where the letter was placed in his hand, and the door shut in his face. Barto rushed to him, but Luigi, with a vixenish countenance, standing like a humped cat, hissed, "Would you destroy my reputation and have it seen that I deliver up letters, under the noses of the writers, to the wrong persons?—ha! pestilence!" He ran, Barto following him. They were crossed by the officer on horseback, who challenged Luigi to give up the letter, which was very plainly being thrust from his hand into his breast. The officer found it no difficult matter to catch him and pluck the letter from him; he opened it, reading it on the jog of the saddle as he cantered off. Luigi turned in a terror of expostulation to ward Barto's wrath. Barto looked at him hard, while he noted the matter down on the tablet of an ivory book. All he said was, "I have that letter!" stamping the assertion with an oath. Half-an- hour later Luigi saw Barto in the saddle, tight-legged about a rusty beast, evidently bound for the South-eastern gate, his brows set like a black wind. "Blessings on his going!" thought Luigi, and sang one of his street-songs:—

"O lemons, lemons, what a taste you leave in the mouth! I desire you, I love you, but when I suck you, I'm all caught up in a bundle and turn to water, like a wry-faced fountain. Why not be satisfied by a sniff at the blossoms? There's gratification. Why did you grow up from the precious little sweet chuck that you were, Marietta? Lemons, O lemons! such a thing as a decent appetite is not known after sucking at you."

His natural horror of a resolute man, more than fear (of which he had no recollection in the sunny Piazza), made him shiver and gave his tongue an acid taste at the prospect of ever meeting Barto Rizzo again. There was the prospect also that he might never meet him again.